John Poyer

St. Thomas à Becket and other poems

John Poyer

St. Thomas à Becket and other poems

ISBN/EAN: 9783337206321

Printed in Europe, USA, Canada, Australia, Japan

Cover: Foto ©Andreas Hilbeck / pixelio.de

More available books at **www.hansebooks.com**

St. Thomas à Becket:

AND OTHER POEMS.

BY

JOHN POYER,

AUTHOR OF " ANTI-COLENSO," ETC.

"A thing of beauty is a joy for ever."—KEATS.

LONDON:

EDWARD MOXON & CO., DOVER STREET.

1865.

LONDON :

BRADBURY AND EVANS, PRINTERS, WHITEFRIARS.

TO MY WIFE.

To her I met in manhood's dawn,
And seeing gave my soul in love ;
To her by whom I then was drawn
With mystic notes of cooing dove :

To her who fill'd my trancèd eye,
A vision of the higher light,
And brought the radiant Heavens anigh
And vocal made the stilly night :

To her whose form of maiden grace
Did waft my thought to Eden's streams,
And gave this Earth its olden face
When Eve with angels talk'd in dreams :

And drew from shining Worlds afar
A life deep wed to love and song ;
Where silent is all storm of war,
And Music walks the summer long :

To her to whom I join'd my life,
As stream that seeks deep Ocean's tide :
And bound her to my heart as wife,
To cross as one Earth's desert wide :

To her as interfused in thought,
And mingled more in fount of fire,
These songs are given as texture wrought
By pulsing sweetness of her lyre.

CONTENTS.

III.

CUM RISÛ.

PROLEGOMENA.

—— ◆ ——

THE NINETEENTH CENTURY, in whose latter half the Historic movement is now pulsating with portentous auguries, has been appropriately designated the "Iron Age." The rigid and intense materiality of iron is in fact precisely the symbol by which its distinctive physiognomy may most truly be formulated. We have not only iron roads and iron guns as never before, but we fear, notwithstanding a seeming paradoxical chivalry obtruded upon the surfaces of society, we have in our high progress arrived at essentially iron manners. The iron hath transcended its own legitimate sphere, and by some strategic force ingeniously brought into play, it hath encroached upon—nay, boldly usurped—the immaterial realm of mind. The iron has entered into our souls. What, it may be asked, is our private and public life in this fond Epoch but an universal attestation to the active presence of Vulcan Redivivus, the force-god— the hero of Iron? Yes, it is even so. Force is becoming increasingly every day the god of this World,

B

and Iron is its symbol and embodiment. Said the
uncle of the astute man across the narrow sea where
"the empire is peace"—"Victory is always with the
big battalions." And he but uttered the faith of the
majorities. Clearly moral heroism is fast becoming a
small thing. The true excellence henceforth must be
held to attach to the new force of the age, the Iron-
power.

In the forthcoming essay, however, we are only
interested to take cognisance of this popular deity in its
relations with literature, and with poetry in particular.
And we will say at once that we shall contend throughout our argument that this inflexible hardness which
is the natural attribute of iron has very extensively
permeated our national literature; yet with this exception, that in the realm of fiction, where its influence
had been beneficial if applied, it has been almost
exclusively withheld, so that the phenomenon now
presented in that field is the exclusive predominance of
the sensational novel as the breath of all aspiration—
the aim of all achievement. The *littérateurs* who now
command large and rapid fortunes are the men happily
not largely endowed with intellect or imagination, who
hysterically throw off their sensational writings in the
flying hour, while they endow them with the agreeable
property of modifying somewhat, though in a very
morbid way, the hard and dry tenacity superinduced
upon the soul by the aforesaid domination of the force-
god.

Nor do we advert to this with the most distant notion that our protest will have any appreciable operation upon this state of things. We conceive the pathological condition of the body-politic in this respect is such that the plenary action of the Divine Spirit alone is adequate to meet and relieve the evil. Yet has the question a prospective reference to the main body of our argument, and we therefore speak to it in passing on.

But we intimated just now that even Poesy was not exempt from the deterioration of this materialising hardness of the Iron-god. Even Poesy, that mode of spiritual being which, if it is true and real, constitutes man the present inheritor of two worlds—the temporal and the eternal—is fast succumbing to the repulsive action of this gigantic and all-embracing Iron-force. We are said to be favoured among other novelties with the presentment of that phase of ethical life which is known as "muscular Christianity;" nor are its lineaments, it would seem, pre-eminently attractive. We conceive that, co-existent with this intensely realistic and frigid innovation, we have presented to us a hard, dry, inflexible, highly materialised prosaic poetry. As we write this sentence there lies open on our library table a volume entitled "Dramatis Personae," by Robert Browning. Well, we will adopt this book as the text of our argument, and we say fearlessly, and without any doubt whatever, that, with here and there an exception, it is a book of mere hard, dry, broken iron sentences

with scarcely a poetic element in the entire fabric from
end to end.

We sometimes find the realistic Englishman in a
highly exacerbated mood, railing at what he intelligently
proscribes as "German transcendentalism." We are
curious to know what may be the attitude of such a
critic to the writings of Mr. Browning, and to this book
in particular. Does he really persuade himself that he
is moving in a realm either of light or of beauty? Is
he really sweetly travelling in the high and glorious
region of ideal Truth which is for evermore the true
sphere of poetic representation? We do not hesitate to
say that Kant's Critique of the Pure Reason is light and
beauty itself as compared with the dark and dismal
sentences of the "Dramatis Personae." In Kant, if you
have a somewhat cumbrous terminology, you certainly
have consecutive thought delivered in a logical and
unbroken series, so that in virtue of the analogies of
mind, you can have no difficulty in apprehending his
meaning throughout his argument; but we defy any
one, be his intellectual force what it may, to interpret
Mr. Browning upon any known principles of logical
thought or grammatic structure. At any rate, if there
are persons in the round world who really find themselves equal to this high achievement, we conceive they
must be gods certainly, not men. We find only in the
book a monstrous medley of broken, inarticulate utterances—a rude inorganic mass of disjointed conceptions,
chiefly strangled in the very act of birth. In short, we

can only interpret his mind at all upon the basis of its
analogical relation to a broken mirror, from which all
power of convergence is utterly departed. Of course, as
we are writing an original essay, and not a review, it
will not be deemed obligatory upon us that we should
formally prove the point stated by citation and analysis,
though nothing were easier than to exhibit in detail
the truth of the representation. We proceed with our
main subject.

It is now somewhat more than fifty years ago when
Wordsworth inaugurated a new epoch in the sphere of
poetic literature. Conceiving, as he seems to have
done, that in the course of time the language by which
poetic thought is conveyed had become fantastic and
unreal—that it stood antithetically opposed to the
mode of utterance commonly employed in everyday life—
he arrived at the conclusion that it was his distinctive
mission to emancipate the world from what he apprehended to be æsthetically a great and growing evil. He
seems to have thought that while in the early rise of
poetry the figurative language, then ordinarily used in
all poetic representation as that proper to be used for
the utterance of passion, was legitimately applied, yet
now, in these later degenerate times, poets had no right
any longer to employ this kind of diction, for that it
was perfectly palpable it had ceased to retain its aboriginal vitality. The imagery, indeed, was left, he
thought, but the passion, which was its life and energy,
had passed away, and this being so, he argued that

henceforth poets must be content to restrict themselves
to the language of everyday life, for that thus only
would they be true to themselves and intelligible to the
world. Says he, in the essay in which the new canon is
enunciated :—" It may be safely affirmed that there
neither is nor can be any essential difference between
the language of prose and metrical composition."
Well, upon this assumed axiom, as we now all know,
Wordsworth proceeded with infinite labour and pains to
construct that stately edifice by which his fame will
deservedly descend to future ages. He contended
strongly for the use of common language, and he
adhered rigidly for the most part in practice to the
theory which he had postulated.

Now, while cherishing Wordsworth's memory with
high regard, we utterly dispute his doctrine. We can
perfectly understand the ground and cause of its origin,
but we think the time has come when it must be sub-
mitted to such analytic scrutiny as will test its nature
and character, and ascertain how far it is really
accordant with the deep and eternal laws of the human
mind. The occasion of the genesis of the new canon
we apprehend to lie in the relatively vapid writing of
many of his cotemporaries—poets who wrote fine and
fluent verses—pleasant to the ear and generally stimu-
lating to the sense, but presenting little substantive
support, whether to the reason or to the imagination.
Nor must Pope himself, the reputed master of the then
received school, be supposed to be excepted to Words-

worth's proscription, for if his verses are pre-eminently
smooth and elegant, as they undoubtedly are, the
thought and sentiment underlying and creating their
organic structure are as unquestionably poor, meagre,
and unsatisfactory. The age of Wordsworth impera-
tively demanded a higher and a more generous aliment,
and Wordsworth no doubt exerted himself nobly, and
with considerable success in the end, to meet and satisfy
the longing.

But we referred also to the cause of this new intellectual movement, and this we think is explained by
the peculiar idiosyncracy of Wordsworth's own mind.
It is evident, we think, from the whole scope and tenor
of Wordsworth's writings, that the quality of passion
which is the motive power of all high poetry was
relatively dormant in him, and that his thought is
evermore moving in the calm reflective sphere of the
reason, kindled to some extent, though not largely, by
the creative imagination ; so that, as in such case must
be the necessary consequence, we are entertained by
him rather with ethical disquisition interblended with
biographical incident, than with the genuine creations
of the poetic faculty. We conceive the " Excursion "
forcibly exhibits the truth of this representation.
Thus, then, Wordsworth wanting the force and the
fervour of passion, unconsciously framed a doctrine
that, while it adequately represented the peculiar form
of his own mind, is not found to be co-extensive with
the full-orbed intellect, and not adequate to satisfy

whether the lofty function or the boundless aspiration
of the poetic art.

To contend, as he does, that the language of Poetry
is homogeneous with that of prose, and that poets must
be content to forswear and forsake that figurative diction upon which they have relied in all ages as the only
vestment in which they could even approximately clothe
the celestial inspirations of the Divine Spirit, is, as we
think, profoundly to misconceive both the nature and
the function of the poetic faculty. For the question of
language implicitly involves the higher and the deeper
question of the life of which language is but the symbol
and exponent.

But the life with which Poesy is concerned, is
certainly not the prosaic life of the world in its daily
ebb and flow, save, indeed, as in any case it receives and
reflects that higher life which is consentaneous with the
harmony and the beauty of the inner Heavens. For
Poesy, as we apprehend it, is the intuition of the
spiritual and eternal in the physical and temporal.
With Plato, it contemplates all things under the form
of eternity. With the true poet, Nature and Humanity
are beauteous hieroglyphs of the Godhead ; so that in
every movement of poetic thought the essential thing
before the mind is the inner substance underlying and
sustaining the majestic continuous flow of this mystic
twofold life. The poet looks ever to see the spiritual
forms of things, and so to invest them with that high
ethereal beauty which they are found intrinsically to

possess when transfigured by the imagination in its
penetrative energy transpiercing the grosser sense—they
appear in the light of eternity itself. Thus, in a
measure, the poet anticipates, though it may be feebly,
the glorious effulgence of the beauty which supremely
dominates all things in the bright worlds which gleam
afar in the celestial spaces.

And, as in Nature, so in his relations with Man, the
poet seeks equally the permanent in the transient. He
knows well, that if man is sown in weakness he shall be
raised in power; and all his concern is to take hold of
those beauteous lineaments of our redeemed humanity
which attest the intrinsic aboriginal dignity of our
nature, and show the glorious presence of the Christ
working in His secret but powerful energy to raise up
and emancipate the Race from the ruins of the Fall.

But if Poetry exists to the one end, that it may
witness to the fact and presence of the Spiritual World
encompassing us about, and that it may, in some good
degree, interpret to man the nature and character of its
transcendent life; the distinctive feature of which is,
that it is free and joyous, with the very breath of God—
that it is permeated with the light and beauty of the
Holy Trinity; then it must be conceded that Poetry
must necessarily be endowed with a form of language
which shall be adequate, to some extent, to represent
the high ethereal character of this spiritual and eternal
life: but this language certainly cannot be, as Wordsworth contends, the common speech of every-day life.

For this mode of speech is related only to the practical life which it represents. The language and the life are inextricably bound up in each other, and by a subtle law of causation, which governs their relations and determines their reciprocal interaction, they move continuously, and by an inexorable necessity, upon the same plane of being. They are respectively of and from the world, and their form can only be worldly too. How can it be logically upheld, that the language which utters the words of man in his external relations with society—that is wholly conversant with things of civil life, or state polity, can be an adequate exponent of that higher life of man which is spiritual and ideal. It cannot be. The divine life in man, with which only Poetry is concerned, cannot be uttered in its higher intellectual movements in this language of common life; for the life itself, being diverse in respect of this, its whole organism, intellectually considered, being constructed of immaterial ideas, it is palpable that the language in which its thought shall be clothed must partake its essence and reflect its modes.

Until Wordsworth ventured to call this in question, the poets of all time, in any case where the language of common life failed to utter their thoughts, had recourse to the wider and deeper language which is yielded by terms taken in a figurative or analogical sense. And they had a perfect right to use language precisely in this way. For the whole field of Nature, in all its sights and sounds—the glorious play of its manifold lights—

the rich music of its varied vocal utterances, is strictly
analogous at every point to the soul of man; while
this, in all the complex diversity of its wondrous and
transcendent life, stands for evermore in the most
intimate analogy with the very life of the Godhead.

And this being so, the language of analogy is the
proper, and, as it were, the native language of all high
Poetry; for it is the only language which will convey
poetic thought in its inspired moments: when kindled
by the fire of passion it soars at will in the immea-
surable azure, and sweetly and nobly discourses to man
of the spiritual and eternal, which only are essentially
the good, the true, and the beautiful. We venture,
then, once again, to demand that the language of
analogy be reinstated as the true form of poetic
diction—analogy, however, taken in its intensely vital
and dynamic energy.

And now, we pass on to another point. It has, from
Aristotle downwards, been received as the definition of
Poetry, that it is an imitative Art, whose essential
function it is to please the soul. We venture to contro-
vert this dictum in both its aspects. Poetry is said to
be an imitative Art, for that it represents, through the
medium of language in epos or drama, the past life of
man as recorded in human annals or preserved by
traditionary legends. The thought and passion of man
is revived, and made by the poetic Art to re-appear
from athwart the dim veil which separates between
those of us who are in the flesh and our fellows who

have passed into the great World of Spirits : and this
mode of representation, according to Aristotle, and
those who repeat him, is defined to be a species of
imitative Art, and nothing more. What a miserable
and superficial view of the subject is this! Why even
History is endowed with a higher function than is
implied here. For the muse of History must not only
gift men to read aright the great facts of human life in
their outer semblance, but endow them who undertake
the high and arduous task of interpreting such action
with the finer faculty of intuitively seizing upon the
inner springs thereof by that subtle induction which
conducts the mind into the realm of causation.

And shall it be said that Poetry, forsooth—that is
ideal in its very essence, and for ever remains ideal in
the whole scope of its spiritual movement—is to be
restricted to imitating the past life of the World,
whether in epic narrative or dramatic representation ? Of
lyric utterance, we do not here speak, for it is essentially
subjective and ideal. Its sphere is purely the dynamic
and creative one. But, as it respects the other region
of Poetry referred to, it seems to us that the imitation
theory is utterly incommensurate with the reality of the
case. The poet, it is true, represents by language in
epos and drama the past life of man ; but he does this
subject to the inexorable law, that he shall freely blend
the form of his own being with the very life which, in
any given instance, he is reproducing.

The old maxim of antiquity, that the mode of the

recipient governs all reception, is one that applies to the play of the poetic energy in a deeper and wider sense than to any other form of intellectual effort ; for that the poet, by the very law of his being as such, is from first to last a maker, or creator, and nothing else. That moment in which he ceases to create, he ceases to act as the genuine poet. And if this be so, it must be evident that in representing the thought and passion which have taken incarnate form on the theatre of the world, he cannot but interpret it under the dominating influence of his own idiosyncratic nature. The imitation theory is plausible, indeed, as was its original inventor ; but it is equally shallow and inadequate, and must be relegated to that past to which it intrinsically appertains.

Pass we on to glance at the other aspect of the Aristotelian theory which postulates pleasure as the end or aim of the poetic art. This proposition undoubtedly is far more apparently true than that already disposed of. Yet are we confident that it will not bear the test of a close analysis. It is just as true as the fundamental maxim of the Epicurean Philosophy, which founds upon the assumption that pleasure is the chief good of man. But in each of these cases there is a confusion of substance and accident—of cause and effect—of motive and experience. We hold that the realization of *being*, which is the life of God in the soul, is the sole end of all true life ; and that poetry and philosophy in particular exist in the world for no other purpose than to witness

to and expound this sublime and far-reaching doctrine.
Truth or reality is the necessity of man's nature. He
may, as God pleases, prosecute the great tragic journey
of life with but a small and intermittent allowance of
pleasure as he climbs the arduous steeps of his ascending pathway, but he cannot rest day or night saving as
his soul takes firmly hold of the eternal truth of things.
Inheriting into a nature that although transitorily
clouded, is yet homogeneous with the light of God's
Spirit, he can only live, and he deeply knows it, in the
ratio in which he moves in consentient harmony with
the movement of the great universe. But in order to
this he must live and act in the sphere of Being or
reality, for out of this there is only dissonance and
unrest, and he has no firm basis for his foot, no reposeful
centre for his heart's best affections.

Still though, as we contend, pleasure is no more the
end of Poetry than it is of Philosophy ; yet this blessed
and joyous experience of the soul flows inevitably, even
as an effect from its cause, out of the free play of the
poetic, and, in a less degree, of the philosophic energy.
Pleasure in short is, in a sense, the atmosphere of truth,
and as it partakes its essence so it reflects its joy and
beauty. And inasmuch as Poetry is not only the utterance of ideal truth, considered as bare reality, but the
presentation of the real and permanent in the form of
beauty, and under the condition that all its language
shall be rhythmical in its flow, so as to convey also the
charm of music in the utterance : it undoubtedly is

the case that an ineffable pleasure accompanies all high
and genuine Poetry just as it does the heavenly strains
of Mozart, or any other great master of musical harmony.

And because pleasure is invariably found to grow out
of all Poetry that is worthy of the name, it has happened.
we presume, that Aristotle's ruling has prevailed up to
the present hour, and has been accepted as that special
attribute which is supposed distinctively to mark the
genius and function of the poetic faculty.

In bringing these introductory observations to a conclusion, we would venture a word or two having more
immediate reference to the Poems which it is sought to
introduce to the reader's thoughtful and, we hope.
sympathetic notice in this preliminary essay.

We have been strongly impressed for some time past,
as may be concluded from the gist of our opening observations, that Poetry and Music, although, as we conceive, essentially bound up in each other, are becoming
in this hard utilitarian age increasingly severed.

And in the few observations which we felt constrained
to make in the outset upon the peculiar character of
Mr. Browning's poetry, our chief aim was to signalise
this palpable fact. It must, we think, be evident to all
who care to reflect upon the subject, that Mr. Browning's poetry does not fulfil the laws which govern poetic
utterance. In the first place, proceeding inductively,
we think it must be evident that there is no such thing
as musical rhythm discoverable in the whole body of

his discoursing; or if there be such rhythm, it is the wild intonation of some primitive shepherd's reed, and by no means the graceful and finished harmony of Apollo's lute, evermore sounding in pleasing accompaniment to the rich emotional gurgling of the Pierian Springs.

Then, secondly, the poetry does not seem to proceed as poetry is bound to do, from the emotional centre of our nature. As we are affected by Mr. Browning's poetry, it seems only to be a broken utterance of the hard, dry intellect "done" into a certain wild and abrupt measure, which in itself has only a very distant relation to the musical and harmonious flow of the genuine poetic numbers. But, thirdly, the most lamentable feature in this abnormal and exceptional poetry is its emphatic and repulsive cynicism. To us it seems to come chiefly clothed in the sable garments of the tomb. It is the poetry of death and despair, not of life and joy; a poetry full of the harsh discords of a vain and scoffing world, and with little or nothing of the great epic life which, through all the darkness and tempest of the night, is struggling upward to God and His Angels—to Christ and His redeemed of all times and places.

If our judgment should be proved to be unsound, we can only say that we shall be willing, and indeed thankful to see it set aside. For we would not consciously or lightly detract from the just reputation of any writer, dead or living. But in the great conflict of which this tragical world is the present theatre, we conceive it is the

imperative duty of every man to witness to the truth as
he apprehends it, without fear or favour, in calm,
dispassionate earnestness, looking ever before and
after.

We had intended saying a few words about the
Poems now offered to the literary public, but our limits
are already passed. We will briefly say, that in the
poetry now first presented to the world we have sought,
in accordance with the canons we have propounded, to
give utterance to ideal truth, and to do it musically.
Thus, while seeking in the poems to illustrate the
doctrine stated, that truth or reality is the end as it is
the essence of Poetry, we have not been unmindful
that beauty, which is the form and colouring of truth,
and rhythmic sound, which is the proper voice of truth,
must be included in the representation, so as that joy,
which is most properly apprehended as the witness and
exponent of this poetic truth, may become the posses-
sion of all who may care to relate themselves to the
strains of the lyre which may now give out what sweetness may be there.

Deeply conscious are we that the strain is poor and
feeble when considered in relation to that high and
glorious harmony which floweth down from the seraphic choirs. Yea, it is a weak and a broken utterance, yet hath it sought in some humble measure
to echo the delicious music evermore proceeding from
the crystal sea before the eternal throne. To Christ
and His saints, both in the Church and in the great

broad human World, we desire to present the work as a song of hope, and joy, and love, that looketh to the morning soon about to break upon the Race.

LONDON,
  November 4, 1864.

I.

CUM SALTU.

ST. THOMAS A'BECKET.

PART I

WHERE London fair appear'd in olden time,
Nor dreamt could be the monster of to-day,
When leafy sounds did mingle with its chime,
And sung gay troubadours their wooing lay ;

Where grassy meads did intersect the plain,
And carolled sweet the birds about the eaves,
And rural joy, that cometh not again,
Did freely enter with the golden sheaves :

When gurgling sounds of brooks the ear did charm,
And low of herds went up the stilly night,
And distant was the factory-bell's alarm,
And smoke had not as yet shut out the light :

When commerce plied the tasks by which it rose
In spirit more akin to growth of soul,
And freedom was not buried in the snows,
And kindred bonds did all the place control :

E'en now, when Norse and Saxon blent their life,
And made "one music" in a quiet home,
And gleam'd no more in air the awful knife,
But lyric song and prayer went up the dome:

In this fair place, at this sweet olden time,
In pleasant Cheap a merchant's house did stand ;
A babbling brook anear with shading lime,—
A stately merchant's house in merchants' land.

There, in that goodly house, one stormy night,
When swept the angry blast the sleeping plain,
A wond'rous babe came down the darksome light,
His heralds wailing wind and flowing rain.

There woke from heavenly sleep A'Becket's child,
There came he mid that elemental roar,
There 'gan his course upon this howling Wild,
There Angels to him oped Earth's tragic door.

Conspired the ardent East to build his frame,
For flow'd the Syrian sun within his veins ;
Conspired the Pleiads sweet to form his name,
While Love came with him from the Syrian plains.

For had his gentle mother met his sire
In that fair land of Poësy and Love,
E'en there the twain did own the melting fire
Down-flowing from celestial breasts above.

And when, as Time flew on unresting aye,
And sought again the sire the distant West,
When Chivalry recoiled in baffled way,
And knights who'd striven long did sigh for rest,

The Syrian maid, drawn on by mighty Love,
All fearless crossed the widely-severing sea,
Constrain'd to seek how now her lover throve,
And if he treasured still her ministry.

So came she where old London rear'd its head,
With little knowledge where her Gilbert hid :
Thought she, his name all needful light would shed :
Nor was her hope unbless'd, for so it did.

Thus came she all athwart the mighty sea,
This gentle damsel from far Syria's plain,
And reach'd the famous City of the Free,
And Gilbert found—nor were they longer twain.

So mingled East and West their potent ray,
And fire and light one confluent stream became,
And Becket's name did sunnier make the day,
As swiftly clomb this Child the heights of fame.

Where Merton opes its wide and fertile plain,
And all embower'd doth lie mid shady trees,
And drink its grassy meads the bounteous rain,
And haunt its honey'd sweets the murmurous bees;

There, in the princely Abbey now no more,
Withdrawn from all distracting sight and sound,
A'Becket fed his soul with boyish lore,
And lofty nursed the dreams which spurn the ground.

There Childhood ripen'd into ardent Youth—
There oped his soul as opes the budding flower,
As seeketh *it* the light, so sought he truth,
And sweetly came and went the golden hour.

And when to riper years the boy up-grew,
And Thought began to claim its kingly throne,
To bank of Isis and of Seine he flew,
Where do the Muses share a wider zone.

There with a deeper thirst he drank the stream
Which as a living water feeds the mind;
There with a richer light his soul did gleam,
And formed he higher counsels for his kind.

At famed Bologna next is Becket seen,
Resolved the depths of Roman law to sound;
Nor doth he scanty knowledge therein glean,
Or fruitless take, as some, that cumber'd ground.

For soon, with high commission, sent to Rome
By him who then the nascent Church did rule,
He lustre shed on country and on home,
Great founder known of England's legal School.

His kingly presence, as I see him now,
With eye that lustrous is with service done,
Doth fill me with a sympathetic glow,
While tells it other triumphs shall be won.

There rises calm afore mine inner eye
A'Becket's noble figure in the light,
Erect and tall, with face that seeks the sky,
And smile that chases far the gloom of night.

And now I see the spell of silence broke,
Now flashes subtle wit upon mine ear,
While note I how he charms the common folk,
And how they throng to see and wait to hear.

Accomplish'd, too, in every manly grace,
As knight at arms, or huntsman in the field,
He stood confess'd a leader of the Race,
While held he high and firm Faith's burning shield.

And now his moral height quick saw the king,
And power and rule gave to his steadfast hand ;
And with his fame doth all the kingdom ring,
High Chancellor proclaim'd throughout the land.

And kept he well, I trow, the king's estate,
And highest counsel gave as need up-grew :
Firm held he, too, the royal conscience straight,
And o'er the splendid office radiance threw.

"One heart, one soul," the king and he were found ;
As laughing boys they play'd when work was done ;
Knew not the king as yet dark Envy's sound,
Heard not his inner ear its bitter tone.

And when, as oft it chanced at Becket's board,
Great knights and nobles shared the gorgeous feast,
And flow'd the wine and flash'd the quickening word,
The king was wont to come as of the least.

From chase of stag or boar the monarch came,
And leapt the tables in light joyous way,
Nor conscious seem'd he wore a kingly name,
But freely took as found the festal day.

With friendly hand the loving-cup he took,
And, having drank, would to the field return,
Or sometimes sit with high and piercing look,
While kingly fires did inly flash and burn.

Thus Becket and the king did join their life,—
Thus budding Manhood saw them wholly one ;
All hidden now the sharp and severing knife
That rose anon and woke another tone.

Nor did A'Becket chiefly dwell with Song,
Though Chivalry could find no knightlier man ;
But built he up the State with service strong,
While to uphold the right his message ran.

For did he nobly strive, with thought humane,
The weak and poor to bless, down-trodden long ;—
Fearless he razed the strongholds of the thane,
Where Force long hid the frowning towers among.

And sent he, whence they came, vast hireling bands,
Which long had throve upon the troublous times,
And smiled once more dear England's pleasant lands,
While music pour'd from all the village chimes.

With hand that never falter'd in its hold
He took what had the spoiler seized as prey ;
And gave to whom belonged, possessions old,
And spread o'er hill and dale the sunny day.

And now, ere yet the helm of State he'd quit,
Good service wrought he for the king abroad ;
To knightly prowess join'd he ready wit,
And Gallia show'd where lies high glory's road.

Twice did he cross the narrow belt of sea ;
With regal state he sought the Gallic shore ;
Now Love, now War his lofty ministry,
And Truth his radiant pole-star evermore.

Thus in high service pass'd th' eventful years
In which A'Becket sought the State to raise,
And struggled sunny hopes and darksome fears,
As some his course did blame and some did praise.

PART II.

ALL fiery are the coursers of the Sun ;
With rapid flight they bear the flaming car,
Untiring aye through growing hours they run,
And with them lure the World from Star to Star.

The years revolve, and seasons come and go,
And times that were, oh, come they not again !
And hearts once warm with fire no longer glow,
And what was music once hath lost the strain.

A blinding mist doth wrap us all around,
Nor see we aught in its own proper form ;
Takes all our sight the colour of the ground,
And fill'd is every soul with noise of storm.

And walketh Man all day in idle show,
While drives he balmy peace afar in vain ;
To the dim bourne the silent years do flow,
And cross it ne'er in backward flight again.

Yet through the ceaseless flux of day and night,
'Mid all the changes of the flying year,
Upriseth in the soul a steadfast light
Wherein things lying far are brought anear.

This light now dawn'd in Becket's growing soul,
And did the World another aspect take ;
For was it now the part and not the whole,
And less for more now long'd he to forsake.

And so when Theobald, who loved him long,
Is call'd by Angels to the upper light,
He took his sacred place with prayer and song,
And nobly strove with Chaos and with Night.

High counsel took he with his inmost soul,
When will'd the king to gift him with the trust,
And so he left the part and chose the whole,—
He sought the light and left all meaner lust.

And now to Cantuar bound the trust to take,
A vision met him from the World unseen,
And show'd the might was given for Mercy's sake,
And shed o'er all his soul a golden sheen.

The Primacy he took, and held it well,
High martyr at the last for Christ's dear sake ;
And down the Ages shall his praises swell,
Though all the World combine his fame to shake.

At early dawn he rose with lifted soul,
And sought he strength from Everlasting Hills :
He left the part ; he loved the glorious whole,
Where evermore high Heaven with music thrills.

So did he commune in the morning light
With Him, whose loving Child he'd now become ;
Thus, out of weakness, did he gather might,
While shone far up the Arc his hallow'd home.

With every circling dawn high mass he heard,
And gave himself to Him the Cross who bore,
And wept before the ever living Word,
As more and more He oped Love's golden door.

In such high mood did Becket take the trust,
Which now the king had given to his hand ;
He trod the World beneath him, as the dust,
And sought the Church to spread throughout the land:

The Church, not built with feeble hands of man,
With narrow aisle and darksome roof and low ;
But Church that fair appears as Heaven's wide span—
Where evermore God's Angels come and go:

The Church that is for aye, the living fane
Wherein the Lord doth dwell in light His own ;
The Church that soothes the soul with Music's strain,
And dwells with kingly Christ afore the Throne:

The Church that doth comprise each noble soul
Who loves the right, and inly seeks the true ;
Who leaves the part, and seeks th' Organic Whole,
Where pure and sweet it's seen athwart the blue.

This Apostolic Church, with glory dight,
Sought great A'Becket in the soul to found ;
He sought it in the shade as in the light,
And hallow'd all the search the common ground.

But found he soon the search was well nigh vain :
For did the State absorb the thoughts of men,
The Church nor added fame nor Earthly gain :
The World is *now*—the Church is only *then*.

So did the mighty strife at once begin,
And Church and State a sever'd life was known,—
Sought this, the lower things of Time, to win ;
Loved that, the nobler things beyond, to own.

Dark resteth all the State upon the sand,
With stormy wind and rain about its head,
And swells anon the Flood o'er all the land,
And it is swiftly number'd with the dead.

Reposeth calm the Church upon the Rock,
'Gainst which the waves of Time do strike in vain ;
For is the Kingdom with the " little Flock,"
And shall it cover yet Earth's spreading plain.

So Becket found, however seem'd they one,
And into union ta'en, as things akin,
Their thought and speech did take a diverse tone ;
For look'd the State without—the Church within.

And so with growing might, from day to day,
A'Becket and the king were sever'd found ;
Held firmly each, as chose the separate way,
Nor met they e'er again on common ground.

But how may Poesy express in song
The strife which now the Realm did sorely shake?
How from its golden wings come near the throng,
That 'twixt high Church and State doth question make?

Divergent evermore their path is seen ;
Divergent aye, A'Becket and the king :
And now, when mellow is fair Autumn's sheen,
They meet and talk upon the bitter thing.

Met they where slowly flows the sleepy Nene,
What time in council join'd high knights and lords ;
And fierce and vengeful was Plantagenet seen,
And mean and taunting were his wrathful words.

"Say, were you not," quoth he, "a villein's son,
A chattel on my land, and nothing more ?
What mean these mighty airs you now put on ?
Would thou wert far removed to other shore!"

" Yea, truly, Sire," said Becket, in reply,
" From royal ancestors have I not come ;
Nor was Saint Peter, 'fore me, born thus high,
Yet was he chief, the Apostles bless'd among ;

And e'en to him the Lord of might did give
The mystic keys which Heaven do ope and close ;
For had he own'd the Christ by whom men live ;
For had he well the inner kingdom chose."

" Most true," in haste broke fiery Henry in ;
" But Peter for his Lord, thou know'st, did die."
" E'en so," said Becket, " will I die for Him,
And sweetly to His loving shelter fly.

" When comes the golden hour, oh, puissant king,
And low I hear him call adown the air,
I'll mount and join Him on strong Angel's wing,
Nor shall thy poison'd arrows touch me there."

" You lean too much on that by which you clomb,"
Quoth Henry, now with quick presaging thought :
" Far better were it thou hadst kept at home,
And this thou'lt know ere yet the Battle's fought."

" My trust," said Becket now with sense profound,
" Is not the wretched trust you idly dream,
My trust ne'er yet hath crawl'd upon the ground,
Or ebb'd and flow'd upon a shallow stream.

"For cursed, have I read in Book Divine,
Is every one who puts his trust in Man ;
My trust for evermore is God's and mine,
And doth it dwell for aye beyond thy span.

D

"My trust, oh king! is ever in the Lord,
And He mine head shall guard in Battle's hour;
Lean I upon the Everlasting Word,
When kings do rage and darksome tempests lower."

Thus spake, on bank of Nene, the king and he;
And e'en that sleepy stream awoke to hear;
And went the monarch bound—A'Becket free,
And spread the War through all the mental sphere.

Near to the spot where Sarum lifts its spire,
And points the aspiration of the plain,
There, in high Council, burst the flames of fire,—
There blew the howling wind and fell the rain.

On this historic ground the Council met,—
Met learned clerks and lords the right to try,
Or Church or State to rule; the question set,
E'en this the mighty word that cleft the sky.

Sharp was the conflict seen, and far prolong'd;
Great was the fear that Henry's wrath did raise,
While mailèd barons fierce the Council throng'd,
And strove by threats of sword to win his praise.

With sword and axe, I say, uplifted high,
These valiant men did force the Council there;
With force for wit did they the question try,
For, said they well, "brute force is more than prayer."

And so prevail'd, at last, the royal will,
And strong became the State by strength of law,—
Of law that carries less of good than ill,
And gorges all the day with greedy maw.

With death or exile thrust before their face,
With gleaming brands uplifted o'er their head,
Soon found the clerks they'd joined a futile chase,
So came they all away and left the dead.

Thus Clarendon affirmed the monarch's will;
Thus darkly raised the State its iron shield;
Thus Force smote Freedom with benumbing chill,
And, failing wit, the sword did proudly wield.

Yet tell it not in Gath, or Akka's strand,
How glorious Freedom with the Church did fall:
How mourning then did fill the stricken land,
And grief and terror spread their darksome thrall.

But is A'Becket whirl'd from storm to storm,
While darkens more and more the hanging cloud:
And now base charges his opponents form,
And wrongful dealing feign with clamour loud.

By that dark water where they met afore,
The primate and the king are found again:
There Henry show'd anew his rankling sore,
And scarce from open violence did refrain.

D 2

But Becket, in his priestly garment clad,
At God's high altar brave and strong became ;
From mass came he with aspect calm and glad,
Resolv'd he'd bow alone to Jesu's name.

And to this lofty purpose firm he held,
For did he know the strife was darkly hid,
Nor had his soul for private ends rebell'd ;
The common weal he sought in all he did.

For is the common weal the Gospel law,
And doth the Church exist to make it plain ;
And this A'Becket inly felt and saw,
And nobly strove the object to attain.

But is the common weal confused and dim,
For man loves not his neighbour as his soul ;
His tangled march is led by lust and whim ;
He seeketh aye the part and not the whole.

E'en thus it was with wrathful Henry here ;
The State he view'd as bound in him alone,
And ever was its aspect fair and dear
When it was found to yield him all the throne.

The common weal, ah! then he liked it best,
When with his passing humour it combined ;
When not, its glory faded in the West,—
Nor was it gaily seen with laurel twined.

And Becket inly knew thus stood the case;
And so, when feign'd the king the State to build,
He said "the Church alone could form the Race;
Here must the Nation seek the perfect guild."

And having said, and fail'd the word to found,—
For was he overborne by sword and spear,—
An exile did he roam on alien ground,
Yet with his country ever loved and near.

PART III.

A shadowy land, dear man, this Earth doth show—
A shadowy land it is from year to year;
For o'er it aye the clouds do come and go—
The massive clouds all dark with sorrow's tear.

The storm-clouds o'er it flow with darksome frown,
And sweeps the howling wind the lonesome plain,
And chilly rains do fall the air adown,
And is the soul with 'numbing Winter slain.

Swift withereth the grass in all the field,
And fadeth quick the flower upon the lea,—
At morn a vernal aspect do they yield,
At night all sere is grass and flower and tree.

And so as pilgrims only do we wait,
Where clouded is the plain from eve to morn ;
And yet is bound with golden links our fate,
For love hath never left us all forlorn.

As weary pilgrims do we tread the ground,
Far journeying there whence comes the light of day ;
And inly fed do march to Music's sound,
While Kingly Christ doth lead the climbing way.

E'en so doth Becket come to know to-day,
How that he, too, is but sojourner here,—
Comes he to faint along the thorny way,—
Comes he to weep the exile's bitter tear.

And with him went across the sundering sea
The faithful few whom force nor flight could move ;
Nor could the king hold back their ministry,
Nor sever them who long were knit in love.

When Winter's chilly wing was on the air,
And wailing voices came adown the wind,
Went they undaunted forth in love and prayer,
And show'd how its own place is aye the mind.

For is the mind of noblest essence free,
And doth it grandly move in realm its own,
And is its sweep majestic like the sea,
And doth it reign alone from zone to zone.

So Becket left the king the State to form;
Thrust out for that he check'd despotic will,
And calm withdrew he from his 'vengeful storm,
And took the martyr's cup of present ill.

Pontigny saw him touch the Gallic shore,
And shelter nobly gave him, stricken low,
And for the same is hallow'd evermore,
While shineth all the place with sunny glow.

There came A'Becket on Saint Andrew's day,
And left the wayward World its path to take,
And took his soul the mystic inward way,
And dwelt with Thought and Love by peaceful lake.

There in the inner realm of mind he dwelt,
And strove by thought to reach the depths of life;
There, too, before the Holy One he knelt,
While saw he from afar Hate's gleaming knife.

In studies of the Book from Heaven sent down,
By which the soul to angel heights doth grow,
A'Becket lives,—nor heeds the monarch's frown,
Nor asks how doth the World or ebb or flow.

Thus many days did silent come and go,
And furious storm'd the king athwart the sea;
And Becket's friends smote he with frenzied blow,
Yet could he not control the spirit free.

And now to Vezelay did A'Becket haste,
What time high Whitsuntide did crown the year;
There drove he out his foes into the waste,
And spread o'er all the land a rending fear.

There in the Abbey Church he stood and cried,
And with prophetic utterance pour'd his ire;
Nor from the curse could they or fly or hide,
Whom now the prophet search'd with judgments dire.

They vex'd and spoil'd the Church with ruthless hand,
And chose the part, and spurn'd the glorious whole,
And brought an iron rule upon the land,
And now must know the Church doth still control.

For is the Church supreme in realm of mind,
And giveth there the law that rules the World:
While is the State to lower things assign'd—
For is it aye by earthly passion whirl'd.

So, excommunicate are now the men
Who rent the seamless robe that clothes the Race;
Oh! happy they, if reunited then,
When Christ, as king, shall show his glorious face.

And now the king, though Becket pass'd him by,
Content to urge him to a better mind,
Is swiftly fill'd with resolution high,
That he no more shall peaceful shelter find.

And so, by threats like those oft used before,
Where now at Citeaux met who Becket loved,
The king expell'd him from Pontigny's door,
And he, once more, the homeless exile roved.

So, 'mid the tears of them who loved him there,
For that they saw the grandeur of his soul,
He left the place with flowing love and prayer,
To Christ still bound as needle to the pole.

And here it was, when now about to go,
A troublous vision smote him in the night;
And so was all his movement sad and low,
While dim and drear appear'd the morning light.

For had he seen athwart the veil of sleep
A spacious temple open on his sight,
With Pope and Council in the airy deep,
And swords portentous in the awful night :—

For had he seen that Council rent in twain,
And eke himself contending warmly there,
While by four knights he's borne away and slain,
Though had the Pope with favour heard his prayer.

And so foreshadow'd thus his tragic end,
A'Becket left Pontigny's friendly shade,
And to Columba's House his way did wend,
And found he there a like consoling aid.

A Benedictine House near Sens it stood,
And open'd wide its doors to take him in,
And gave the love that's sweeter far than food,
And goeth far to heal the wound of sin.

Here, then, by favour of the Gallic king,
A'Becket shelter found from Henry's ire;
While in the night God gave him still to sing,
And brighter burn'd love's sacred altar fire.

Here sought he, still unmoved, the Church to build—
The Church as in her inner beauty seen,
Which grasps the Race as one Organic Guild,
And is for aye of souls the rightful queen.

From Sens went Becket out to meet the king,
With high desire sweet peace to see again;
Twice did he seek to reach the blessèd thing,
And twice did he return all inly slain.

For strove the king his wayward will to keep—
"To save the kingdom," e'er his specious word;
But was not Becket found as one asleep—
"To save the Church," he said, "and own my Lord."

"Saving the Church," said he, "I yield thee all;
And doth the Church the kingdom all include;
But is the kingdom none when *it* doth fall,
And all the State is barbarous and rude."

So held they still two widely separate ways—
Two streams they were that ne'er might confluent be;
So pass'd in futile hopes the weary days,
While ever roll'd between the stormy sea.

The roaring sea with billowy wave was there,
And Time did with the Timeless strive in ire;
Yet mingled, too, sweet voices in the air,
And streamèd down the arc celestial fire.

PART IV.

Oh! beauteous on the silent mountain height,
Are aye the feet of them who whisper peace,—
Who cheer with song and love Earth's lonesome night,
And from sweet Charity do never cease;

Whose lips the living coal hath touch'd with fire,
And all whose utterance is the breath of love,—
Whose very anger is a righteous ire,
Downflowing from celestial breasts above;

Who, charged with high commission from the Lord,
Do soar on wings of Faith above the World,
And steadfast hold the high prophetic word,
While o'er them is Christ's banner fair unfurl'd;

Who pass from strength to strength athwart the deep,
Where moveth aye the World in treacherous hate,
And in the end do sweetly pass in sleep,
And wake where comes no more the gloom of fate.

But is their martyr-life grand epic found,
Discoursing stately music all the night,
Ascending aye above the groaning ground,
Far reaching e'er to Him the Light of light.

Oh! sweet and blest are these thus martyr-led,
To live or die content as Christ sees well;
The living they alone where all are dead,
For only they do His Evangel tell.

And in this army of the King of kings,
Whose march is evermore where Truth doth lead,
A'Becket grandly soars on golden wings,
While 'fore him bends the World e'en as a reed—

E'en as a reed that's shaken with the wind
Doth bow the World before the man of God;
For can it not hold back the flow of mind,
Or sterile make at will the budding rod.

So at the last Plantagenet yielded ground,
Or feign'd the king the irksome thing to do;
For had he not a true repentance found,
Nor did the kiss of peace the courtiers view.

At Freteval met once more the lofty twain,
In place e'en then as " traitor's meadow " known—
Here Church and State awoke the slumbering plain—
When spake they now it seemed in friendship's tone.

No word of what at Clarendon befell
Did now from Henry's honey'd lips proceed ;
But said he softly all should be right well,
And Time should seal anon his solemn deed.

Once more secure the exiles might return,
And take, if found, the goods they'd left behind ;
And Becket's soul did gentlier in him burn,
Yet was the monarch's word but empty wind.

Again and yet again met king and clerk,
With aim the peace to fix on surer base ;
But was the mood of Henry cold and dark,
And troublous more and more grew Becket's face.

Thus on a day at Chaumont did they meet,
And hold, as theretofore, momentous talk ;
But still the king withheld all greeting sweet :
Nor could A'Becket see how best to walk.

Quoth wilful Henry here with wistful quest,
" Why will you not e'er do as is my wish ?
The eagle's eyrie aye should be your nest,
With might untold, but grant me only this."

And clearly saw A'Becket what it meant,
And knew in other form 'twas put before ;
For had one said with like insane intent,
When stood th' Immortal on this cumber'd floor :—

"All these things stretching fair from pole to pole—
All these, O Christ, will I now give to Thee ;—
My regent, Thou shalt rule the mighty whole,
Do Thou but bend Thee low and worship me."

At Chaumont, too, it was that Henry said,
When was the doubtful meeting at its end,
How that at Rouen soon he'd raise his head,
Or else 'cross sea where now his way doth wend.

But with presageful thought said Becket now—
"My mind misgives me much that ne'er again
In this life shall we meet; but why or how
This darksome fear I see not clear and plain."

"What!" said the startled king with rising ire,
"Do you e'en for a traitor take me then ?"
"Far, far be that from *you*," quoth he, "O Sire."
So parted they, nor ever met again.

Six days, oh man, saith the prophetic Word,
Six days shalt thou thy toilsome labour do ;
Six years strove Becket 'neath the vengeful sword,
But shall the Sabbath end the weary woe.

Soft blew the southern breeze athwart the sea,
And Becket trod again the English shore,—
And was he met with song and minstrelsy,
For had the People wept his absence sore.

Blessèd, said they, in high exultant strain,
Is he who cometh now in God's own name,
And did they spread their garments in the plain,
And silent were his foes with conscious shame.

With face all flush'd with heavenly joy serene,
A'Becket now into the temple came,
When on the floor was he all prostrate seen,
While in the choir the monks did laud his name.

Said faithful Herbert, seeing their great love,
" Now, oh my lord! need we nor care, nor fear,
How soon the World you leave, and fly above,
For you in Christ are more than Conqueror here."

From choir to chapter-house A'Becket went,
And high discourse there held on words divine,—
" Here have we no continuous city lent,
But seek we one to come, O Lord, e'en thine ! "

E'en such the text from which inspired he spoke,
For was the golden City in his heart ;
Soon would the Sense withdraw its darksome cloak,
Soon would he see the whole, no more the part.

And now A'Becket to his Province come,
Did interlopers turn from out his fold ;
Placed he the exiles in their long lost home,
And to the poor gave freely of his gold.

But was it seen, though active thus for good,
The great ones of the World did come not near;
While Brock, and other foemen fierce and rude,
A'Becket's folk did beat, and kill his deer.

Thus darksome was the sky above his head,
And did the clouds a growing blackness take ;
Seem'd they in symbol form to show the dead,
Who sought in Becket's blood their thirst to slake.

Came on the hallow'd hour of Christmas Eve,
When men and angels join to laud the night,
And choral voices sweetest songs do weave,
And wakeful eyes do watch for morning light.

And with the blessèd time was Becket fill'd,
And in the temple sought he now the Lord,
And with His Generation was he thrill'd,
As did he read it there from out His Word.

With joy he traced the grand historic line
By which the Holy One came down to man ;
And, as he read, did glory in him shine,
Whilst musical and sweet the sentence ran.

The rise of Him, he read, that Holy Child,
Who leadeth back the Race to Eden gone ;
Who gently draws it from the savage Wild,
Nor leaves it till replaced before His Throne.

The sacred night soon melteth into day,
And is A'Becket once more in the shrine,
And doth he show the Saints the golden way
Whereby the steep is clomb to heights divine.

"On Earth calm peace to men of gentle will,"
Was now the sacred text from which he spake ;
And did his burning words his hearers thrill,
And did they weep with him for Christ's dear sake ;

For sweet and lowly Christ, for ever slain
By wicked men who holy peace do hate,
And long have fill'd with slaughter all the plain,
Nor e'er will cease till crush'd by iron fate.

With Becket did they weep, and for him, too ;
For did he show how little peace was loved,
And told how Hate afore there Alphege slew,
And e'er as raging beast to slay it roved.

Then went he on to say that he moreo'er
Would soon the work complete placed in his hand ;
That soon on Earth they'd see his face no more,
For call'd he was away to Morning Land.

E

And hearing this, the People wept anew,
And said, " Why, Father, dost thou leave us so ?
And who shall feed and guide the lonesome few,
When thy dear voice shall cease its hallow'd flow ?"

But he now, changing quick his thought and tone,
(For did the Lion mingle with the Lamb)
Invective pour'd as king on loftiest throne,
And foemen of the Church did boldly damn :

And rightly did he hurl his censure down
Upon the heads of them high law that brake ;
Who base prolong'd the wrathful monarch's frown,
And from the land its sacred peace did take.

Rightly, I say, did he put out of pale
The greedy wolves that in his fold he found ;
For doth the Church ne'er own blind Fortune's gale,—
From Christ it takes and gives all holy ground.

So, then, Nigel de Sackville, get thee gone ;
No right hast thou to show as priest to serve ;
Brute force may not confer the priestly throne,
Nor shall it drive the Church from law to swerve.

The bishops, too, who crown'd the monarch's son,
And had no right of law the act to do,
With lofty ire he censured, one by one,
And o'er his office dazzling splendour threw.

Meantime the wolf of York, one Roger known,
Who evil genius proved afore the king,
With two whom Becket made to walk alone,
Did haste athwart the sea on Fury's wing.

Came they to Bures, where Henry held his Court,
And pour'd the slanderous lie into his ear :
And basely trusted he their vile report,
And furious grew with mingled rage and fear.

Said they—" Sedition 'gins to roam abroad,
For did five horsemen join A'Becket's train,—
Five stranger knights form'd escort on his road,
What time of late he journey'd 'long the plain."

And true it was five knights from London rode,
When late he travell'd backward to his home :
For was their inner house the same abode,
And did they climb with him th' ascending dome.

So heaved the monarch's breast with vengeful ire,
And from the prelates sought he what to do :
Said Roger—" From your barons this inquire :
It resteth not with us the thing to show."

And then with after-thought said this dark man,
" As long as Thomas lives, my lord and king,
No quiet days will you e'er see, or can,
Nor may the State repose with restful wing."

On which the king with hotter fury burn'd,
And strove for voice within him Passion's cry,
And on them flashing eyes he fiercely turn'd,
And madly spake this dark soliloquy.

Quoth he—" A fellow this who ate my bread ;
His heel hath lifted 'gainst my royal crown ;
My grace he scorns, nor honours he mine head,
While doth he trample all the kingdom down.

" This fellow, who into my Court did break,
On stumbling hack, with meagre cloak for seat.
Now swaggers on my throne where all's at stake,
And you look on as though the thing was meet."

Thus darkly spake the king with murderous hate,
And darkly heard him some then present there ;
And in that hour was seal'd A'Becket's fate—
E'en then, when pour'd the king this awful prayer.

Four caitiffs there responded to the call—
Fitzurse, De Morville, Tracy, Brito, known
As men who cow'd beneath a tyrant's thrall—
Seized they the word thus fraught with murder's tone.

Possess'd them as a fiend these awful words,
And drove them day and night 'cross land and sea ;
While all their sight was fill'd with blood-stain'd swords,
Nor could their feet enough with swiftness flee.

Yet all too swiftly did they cross the sea—
Too swiftly came by differing routes to land—
And having join'd, sought Cantuar's smiling lea,
And carried there the ruffian's coward brand.

Meantime the king, mistrusting what he'd done,
A council of his barons call'd in haste;
Said—"Becket had as tyrant homeward gone,
And drove his prelates out into the waste;

"That all the country was unquiet made,
And that the clerk would soon dethrone the king
As legate would he place the Crown in shade,
And kings and nobles now must droop their wing."

E'en thus in substance spoke the wrathful king.
And anger kindled he in all the throng;
And Bohun said that "hanging was the thing
For one who'd vex'd so good a king so long."

And did Malvoisin add to help the strain—
"Late told was I, as through old Rome I pass'd,
That e'en a Pope for insolence was slain:"
So cried they all to bind A'Becket fast.

And Mandeville, great Earl, to Quinci join'd,
With one De Humet, too, for sake of law,
Who kept the rod for them who goods purloin'd,
With warrant left all fill'd with hate for awe:

With warrant of the king the three did go
A'Becket to arrest and treason stay—
Eke told the knights to catch, if not too slow,
And hold those hands already raised to slay.

With warrant arm'd they cross'd the narrow sea,
To seize and bind whom nowhere can they find;
For is he gone where calm do live the free—
Where Christ doth reign for aye great King of mind.

So leave we them their search to make in vain,
And backward trace our steps a pace or two,
And look at those there darkening all the plain,
A deed about to work which they shall rue.

From Saltwood Castle are they gone to-day,
And fierce De Broc, its lord, is with them bound;
At Saint Augustine's House, while on their way,
They parley hold ere yet they stain the ground.

But do they hasten to the Palace hall,
Where Becket with his clerks hath pass'd the noon,
And now with talk doth hold them in sweet thrall,
When yet deep instinct told what's coming soon.

And now the miscreants four to Palace got,
With menace claim A'Becket's face to see,
And by a traitor led, as is the lot,
Are named as come from Court across the sea.

So to his presence were they straightway brought,
While high discourse thrill'd all the sacred room ;
And, as it seem'd, with doubts and fears they fought,
For were they silent as the darksome tomb.

Without a word, long gazèd each at each,
These strangers, dark on him and he on them,
Till Becket sought what Tracy had to teach,
Or if he came with purpose to condemn.

Yet still no answer came from them or him,
And seem'd the lofty gift of speech withdrawn ;
When Fitzurse, moved by cold, sardonic whim,
" God help thee " said, and blotted out the dawn.

The dawn, poor fool, he blotted out, I say,
And drew the pall of night upon his soul,
With power no more at morn to sing or pray,
And peace for ever fled from pole to pole.

Once more in silence look'd they each on each,
Till Fitzurse once again the spell did break,
And said that from the king had he brought speech,
And now the same to tell free leave would take.

Whereon, in harsh and inarticulate sounds,
He Becket blamed that he the Crown withstood,
And would not stoop to heal its rankling wounds,
While threaten'd he the Realm to bathe in blood.

Feign'd he, moreo'er, the puissant Henry fear'd
How that upon the crowning of his son,
When Becket censured them who interfered,
(But had no right) great mischief had been done.

And did he close his false and idle words
With special charge, said he, borne from the king,
"That you do instant go 'cross Oxon fords,
And fealty yield the son, and end the thing."

To which mad speech A'Becket made reply :
"That, save the king, none loved the son as he,
Who wish'd his royalty might grow more high,
While reign'd he o'er a People brave and free :

"That as to threats, implied or open shown,
What threat could hide within his People's joy,
Who flock'd to meet him now at last come home,
Though not sweet peace to find without alloy ?"

Then next, as to the bishops' case, he said :
"The Pope, not he, had put them out of pale,
And must the lower serve the higher head ;
Yet, pardon ask'd, he'd them as brethren hail.

"If this they'd do, and trial be bound to take,
E'en as is ruled of old by canon law,
Absolvèd they should be for Mercy's sake,
Nor longer feel oppressive dread and awe."

" From whom," now interposed Fitzurse, and said,
" From whom th' Archbishopric do you then hold ? "
" The spiritual from God and Pope my head—
The temporal from King, my liege," he's told.

" Do you not own, then," Fitzurse now rejoin'd,
" That all you hold is only from the king ?"
" Not so," he's told, " the two may not be join'd,
For each from each is quite a diverse thing ;

" To God must render we what He doth claim—
To King yield up what God to him hath given :
Thus only doth man fear the Holy Name—
Thus only doth he climb the steeps of Heaven."

On this the knights, with rage unknightly rose,
And gnash'd their teeth, and threw their arms about :
Yet did not Becket fear dark Passion's throes,
But rose in turn and saw their fury out.

Recoil'd before his calm and steadfast eye
This surging madness from the nether deep ;
Yet rose again, as cloud that veils the sky,
What time the howling wind the plain doth sweep :

So closed in thunderous noise the storm of hate,
With promise of a dark and dire return :
So went the men, close wrapp'd about with fate,
While in their souls demoniac fire did burn.

And now the ruffians gone, miscall'd knights,
A'Becket, rising with the darksome hour,
Did seek his clerks to draw from Hell's poor frights,
And point them where no stormy tempests lower.

Calm and assured his manner was, says one,
As though his foes him to a wedding call'd;
E'en such the call, though hidden in the tone,
And so he knew, for was he not appall'd.

Yea, did he know was this his wedding-day,—
And sweet he felt the dear espousals were,—
And long'd he much to take the nuptial way,
And meet his King and Lord far up the air.

But now loud sounds the axe from outer door,
And is A'Becket told "They're arming fast;"
But doth he calmly say: "That all!   What more?
Then let them arm—they'll weary grow at last."

So sounded on the axe, and terror grew
And fled the clerks and monks with guilty fear;
Yet still to Becket clung the faithful few,—
Among them, Edward Grim, but now come here:

A youthful monk, from Cambridge late arrived,
Where too he'd only gone some days before;
He in that flight nor shared nor yet connived,
For fear'd he not, as they, that thunderous door.

So did he with the rest who stay'd behind,
A'Becket urge, with earnest prayers and tears,
That refuge in the Church he'd aim to find,
For there, thought they, will God allay all fears.

But was A'Becket now from fear borne high,
And willing death to meet where now he stood :
So, prompt and firm, did he refuse to fly;
There, where he was, said he, he'd yield his blood.

Whereon by force they carried him along,
And through dim cloisters bore him to the shrine
Where now fill'd all the place the Vesper song,
And soar'd the soul on wingèd words divine.

And now did Henry of Auxerre come near
(For had Llewellyn gone athwart the sea)
And bore the sacred Cross of blessèd cheer,
And waved it to that lofty minstrelsy.

Anon by northern transept enter'd he,
Whom now did follow they who sought his life ;
Came he as one whom fear could ne'er make flee,—
Look'd he as one who quail'd not at the knife.

And so when saw he some about the door,
In act, as thought to shut red murder out ;
" No fortress is" quoth he, " God's sacred floor,
He knows how best and when His foes to rout."

And added he, " let all come in who will ;"
And forthwith bravely oped the door again ;
And might he, had he chose, have fled their ill,
Who sought to number him among the slain.

But now, though warmly urged, escape to seek,
Would not A'Becket yield a step's retreat,
But to the smiter gave he there the cheek,
And 'fore the Altar sunk his failing feet.

Already had the monks him bore away,
Part up the steps which to the choir did lead,
When Fitzurse from the cloister found his way,
And clamorous grew, as grew his awful need :

So shouted he, now got within the shrine,—
" Come after me, king's men, and follow near ;"
And follow'd near the other three behind ;
But even so much trembled they with fear :

With guilty fear and awful dread they came,
And hideous was the sound of murderous feet ;
More hateful that which call'd A'Becket's name,
And " traitor " dared to add, as fit and meet.

And so, to this foul word no answer came,
But deeper grew the silence of the place,
While dimlier burn'd the faintly flickering flame,
And hidden was the sought but dreaded face.

" Where's th' Archbishop ?" now Fitzurse inquired
Of some poor monk, on whom his hands he laid :
To which, said Becket, now with anger fired,
In voice that sharply cleft the vaulted shade,—

" E'en here am I ! no traitor found or known,
But sacred priest of God do here I stand ;
If me ye seek, ye've found me 'fore His throne :
What would you have ?   What hideth in your hand ?"

At this retreated they in awe and fear ;
And one, as lacking nerve to act, did cry—
" Flee thou ! for art thou dead, and waits thy bier."
" I will not flee," A'Becket said, " but die !—

" Your brutal swords no terror have for me,—
I welcome death in holy Freedom's cause :
I'll die ! and shall the Church be pure and free,
And will I serve my God and keep His laws."

And having said, came he from where he stood,
And 'gainst a pillar firmly set his back,
And waited there while they should shed his blood,
With little thought that pain his flesh might rack.

Thus placed, these brutal men again demand
That he would free whom for their fault he'd bound :
Quoth he, " I'll ne'er relax my steadfast hand
'Gainst them who ne'er repentance sought and found."

Then did they seek to take him captive there,
And press'd they closer to where then he stood ;
But would not great A'Becket grant their prayer :
" Here, as you thirst," said he, " take here my blood."

On this, bold Fitzurse seized his sacred pall,
But Becket threw him off with vigorous hand ;
And Tracy coming at his fellow's call,
Is hurl'd to ground at the swift soul's command :

And Fitzurse now, with fury glowing more,
Did wave his sword above A'Becket's head ;
But was he rapt beyond this darksome shore,
And was his soul with martyr glory fed.

And now, ere yet the mortal blow did fall,
When did they Becket seek to drag away,
Young Grim did bravely hold him to the wall,
And for a time check'd he the murderer's way.

But did bold Fitzurse to his fellows cry—
" Strike ! strike !" and Tracy's sword rose high in air,
And Grim, with cloak on arm, did nobly try
The savage blow to ward, down-coming there.

Yet did he not his generous purpose gain,
Though was his arm disabled with the stroke :
And so with blow on blow the Saint was slain,—
Yet fell not he as they who have no hope.

For then, when gleam'd the blades afore his eye,
And their sharp edge did strike his saintly head,
Said he, " For Christ and His I joyful die,
For they alone do live—the World is dead ;

" And life is that for which my soul doth pant,
But the poor World hath only death to give ;
So will I die it's death to reach my want,
So shall the sword but give me more to live.

" With dear and blessèd Christ my life is hid ;
I go that pearl to seek in higher light ;
By martyr's gate come I, e'en as I'm bid,
And sweet and calm is all this solemn night."

Such requiem sung A'Becket to his soul
In that high moment blent with fading night ;
Thus soar'd he far beyond the World's control,
While boundless stretch'd the radiant zones of light.

Saw he, as ne'er before, the glorious whole,
For which he strove through all his tragic life ;
Knew he the Church would yet attain the goal,
Where should the State not reach with traitor's knife :

The perfect whole, which Love one day shall build—
A living Temple, filling all the sky—
A People that shall be of Christ the Guild,
And with deep wisdom see e'en eye to eye.

This was the vision dawning on his sight,
When call'd his place to take athwart the veil;—
This was the glory that effaced the night,
And pour'd the joy and strength when flesh did fail.

And from thy martyr heights behold us now—
For is thy human love more pure and deep—
Breathe sweetly thou, and tell us when and how,
And with dear Christ and thee we'll wake from sleep.

RICHARD CŒUR DE LION.

PART I.

GREAT Charlemagne ruled the West with mighty hand,
And Genius budded 'neath his fostering sway,
And Franks and Teutons kiss'd the Muses' wand,
And gentle grew before their sunny ray.

And on a day when far his fame had flown
Came one before him from the distant East,
Where then Al Raschid sat on gorgeous throne,
And with his golden rule mix'd song and feast.

A herald came from that great monarch there,
And bow'd him low before this high-soul'd king,
And gave him here the golden keys of prayer
Of that dear fane where weary pilgrims sing.

He brought the keys that oped the sacred door
Where sinful men oft went to weep and pray;
He brought the keys that show'd the hallow'd floor
Where lowly women knelt the night and day.

F

He brought the beauteous keys from that bless'd fane
Where meek-eyed children lisp'd the Holy Name,
And Heaven to Earth did sweetly stoop again,
And give the blind to see, to leap the lame.

And Charlemagne took the keys as guerdon high,
And loved he much their pure and brilliant form,
And oped therewith that Temple of the sky,
And there oft clear'd his brow from cloud and storm.

So Charlemagne took the keys and fell asleep,
And oft athwart the veil look'd on the fane;
Full oft he saw pale pilgrims come and weep,
While moon on moon did swiftly wax and wane.

Through many peaceful years they went and came,
From all the West they stream'd, a gleaming line,
And kindled there love's pure and golden flame,
And took with joy the holy bread and wine.

But now as flew the years in rapid gyre,
And all things changed before their flaming wings,
Did outward burst again the smouldering fire
Which long had slept in view of higher things.

The scorching fire of dark fanatic hate
As lava spread athwart the " Pleasant Land,"
And stamp'd with burning zeal the pilgrim's fate,
Nor stay'd its flow till reach'd the Jordan's strand.

For had the Arab yielded to the Turk,
And brutal Force now strove to reign supreme,
And proved averse to own meek Mercy's work,
And holy Love did count as idle dream.

So Gallic Peter rose from lonely cell,
From realms of silence and the dim unknown ;
Caught he the echoes which the air did swell,
That brought from this far East dark Sorrow's moan.

And thrill'd he in the deeps that note to hear,
And came abroad into the light of day,
And stirr'd in lofty souls great awe and fear,
And lit a flame which burn'd with quenchless ray.

So surged in fiery wave the first Crusade,
By Godfrey high of Bouillon nobly led,
And hid the Seljuk chieftains in the shade
When Chivalry awoke and raised its head.

Around fair Ascalon the battle raged ;
There on the spreading plain the Races strove,
E'en there with battle-axe and lance they waged
Titanic war, and casque and cuirass clove.

And hurl'd the Western Knights their foes to ground
And forced the Holy City from their hands ;
When to the West again they slowly wound,
And Godfrey straightway ruled the willing lands.

Once more the pilgrims sought the holy shrine,
With prayer and song they flow'd from West to East;
Once more they ate the bread and drank the wine,
And join'd in love's high sacrificial feast.

So fifty years ascending cycle made
And carried up the World to higher light,
When kindling Mosul left the realms of shade
And to Edessa came and there made fight.

And fell Edessa's high and bastion'd walls
Afore the mighty sweep of that proud wave,
And wailing voices mourn'd in Western halls,
And gentle eyes did dewy sorrow lave.

And Bernard rapt of Clairvaux heard the cry,
And straight his soul did quiver to the tone;
As wail Æolian harps to evening's sigh,
So thrill'd his heart in Sorrow's plaining zone.

Deep unto deep sent up its tragic song,
As wave on wave swept on in stormy flow;
Soar'd it where dwells the bright angelic throng,
And light and joy exchanged for blinding woe.

So came the great Saint Bernard forth as one
Who held the springs of life within his hand;
Stirr'd he alike the monarch on his throne
And him who marts did seek or till'd the land.

Again the Knights arose with fiery zeal
And kiss'd the sacred cross with burning tears;
'Rom home afar they sought the common weal,
And glory mingled with the flowing years.

Yet did they taste the bitter dregs of guile
From foes in their own house all darkly hid;
The draught Comnenus mix'd in Envy's Isle,
And whom he should have bless'd thus basely chid.

And so to narrow pass of Taurus led
The Teuton bent before the Turkish blade;
And gallant Conrad droop'd his stricken head,
And Chivalry did weep in gloomy shade.

Nor did the seventh Louis better fare
As on Damascus' plain he oped his line,
For sobs of grief did break his evening prayer,
Since they who sang at morn did low recline.

In bonds of death they lie all stark and cold,
And crimson'd is the crush'd and groaning sward;
They ne'er again shall tread the breezy wold,
They're gone at point of lance to God's award.

So ebb'd once more great Knighthood's sacred tide
Afore the surging East it drove in awe,
Till Faith again her lofty gates oped wide,
And Valour saw and own'd high Battle's law.

Once more the years roll'd upward to the Sun,
And with them bore quick thoughts and deeds of man;
In far extending flow they swift did run,
And strove to work the great Redemptive Plan.

And now throughout the young and glowing East
High Selaheddin's name is heard alone,
And nothing heard or seen but song and feast,
While echo all the hills with triumph's tone.

From Egypt lately conquer'd by his arms
Came he elate upon strong Battle's wave,
And Fear before him raised her dread alarms,
Nor could the Franks their tottering kingdom save.

By that sweet lake where once the Blessèd walk'd,
What time poor famish'd souls He princely fed,
And where in loving words divine He talk'd,
And life did give as inmost thoughts He read;—

There on the western bank loud war-cries roar,
There Knights and Templars fell as grass that's mown,—
There Guido lost the Latin Crown he wore,
Nor e'er did win again high Knighthood's throne.

Thus pass'd for aye this kingdom won by sword,
And Selaheddin ruled with mighty hand;
Great chief, of burning soul and quickening word,
He held with iron grasp the " Pleasant Land."

The land and sea athwart the tidings came,
By Tyre's pale bishop brought to trembling Rome,—
Fell Urban e'en as falls the dying flame,
And clouds of darkness folded every home.

PART II.

Yet was there one in Freedom's Isle serene
Whose western edges kiss th' Atlantic wave,
Who bent him not afore the storm, I ween,
Whose hand was quick to strike and strong to save.

There Richard of the Lion-heart up-grew,
Firm rooted as the oak of thousand years;
E'en there as on strong eagle's wings he flew,
And in the depths did leave all gloomy fears.

In knightly deeds he pass'd from youth to man,
With songs reciting war and love he throve;
In valour's lofty field with might he ran,
And coward Falsehood's reign to rend he strove.

So, as the lion strong and brave he grew,
A man of massive build and open brow,
While flowing locks their golden radiance threw,
And show'd the might of Samson's mystic vow.

Flow'd on the news from Rome, all prostrate thrown,
And growing terror stirr'd its course along ;
But Richard seized it from his fearless throne,
And changed the wail to battle's mighty song.

So banners once more flutter'd to the breeze,
Held high, the sacred Cross its myriads drew ;
Again fair Knighthood cross'd broad lands and seas,
And on the East its mail-clad armies threw.

In gallant ships, of Hollander and Dane,
The warriors of the West did proudly sail ;
The sea with joyful song did shout again,
Nor ruffled was its breast with sign of gale.

Met Richard his great rival, France's king,
When fierce the Dogstar burn'd on Vezelai's plain,
And thence to Lyon march'd with spreading wing,
Where sever'd sought the hosts the briny main.

Where Marseille looks athwart the middle sea
That sunders while it joins two mighty shores,
There Richard sought his ships, with spirit free,
Which found not, he to Naples went with oars.

With oars assisting smaller craft he flew,
And reach'd in haste its broad and sunny bay ;
To pleasure there awhile the reins he threw,
And radiant drank Italia's beauteous day.

On fair Salerno next he cast a glance,
And sported gaily with the flying hours ;
There calmly slept his battle-axe and lance,
While Selaheddin sought the coming ghours.

But to Messina's Strait his soul is bound,
And long hath been with silken fetters tied,
There doth he hope to hear love's silvery sound
From one who hastes all blushing to his side.

From proud Navarre doth Berengaria come,
Wise Sancho's daughter, beautiful and sweet,
With grace to deck great Richard's island-home,
And draw high nobles to her beauteous feet.

Where late Italia's hero held his hand,
What time he struck for Freedom's holy law,
And Bomba sought to drive from out the land,
While Naples thrill'd with joy and solemn awe,—

There Richard bounded to the dancing shore,
Expecting long his lithe yet stately tread,—
There met he her to whom his troth he swore,
The Spanish maid whom now he burn'd to wed.

From mountain heights and mountain airs she came,
Where 'mid tall pines wild broom and heather grow,
Where gurgling rills do sing sweet Music's name,
And charm the listening ear with murmurs low.

From Argus' pleasant bank the maiden came,
And left the hills for aye of proud Navarre;
Love bore her, not averse, on wings of flame,
And from dear home and kindred swept her far.

On fair Messina's shore the lovers meet,
And mingle looks and tones that stay my song;
For who may sing or tell how lovers greet,
Who in the pangs of love have travail'd long?

By Faro's Strait their souls together flow,
And blended form a life of richer tone,
With melting heats their quicken'd pulses glow,
Thus sweetly met in Love's electric zone.

With manly pride he kiss'd her virgin lips,
Which, as they ope, the Muses' presence show;
And as the bee, that dewy nectar sips,
So sought he all athirst their honey'd flow.

With secret joy he caught her beaming smile,
Which softly dwelt in eyes of heavenly blue,
Nor fear'd he e'er the traitor's hidden guile
Could lurk in her whom he aspired to woo.

With admiration fond he saw her grace
Commingling with each movement of her frame,
He saw high Beauty thronèd in her face,
Yet could he not pronounce her lofty name.

So there the Lion King Berengaria found
By Faro's water, flowing deep and strong,
There fondly woo'd her to its mystic sound,
As Autumn first, then Winter, swept along.

Beneath Sicilia's azure dome they walk'd,
While queenly Autumn in the woods did reign ;
In Passion's boundless speech entranced they talk'd,
And sounding Faro paused to catch the strain.

And not the less, when Winter stealthy came
And spread his cloudy mantle o'er the scene,
Burn'd bright within their soul Love's deathless flame,
As side by side these lovers there were seen.

But now athwart the sea from Akka swept
The stormy shouts of battle loud and deep,
When from his dreams the Lion-hearted leapt
And at a bound did quit the realm of sleep.

As show'd the Spring in budding leaf and flower,
And life with quicker pulse began to flow,
Felt Richard now had come the solemn hour
When he where Destiny did call must go.

So with a gallant fleet he sailed away,
Nor blue-eyed Berengaria left behind,
A goodly sight old Ocean saw that day
When Richard's sails swell'd out afore the wind.

Yet moon on moon its silvery circle made
Ere yet his eye did greet the Holy Land,
For Cyprus' king a ruthless hand had laid
On some who in a storm had sought its strand.

So Richard, e'er intent high law to hold,
And vindicate its majesty assail'd,
At Limasol did strike with daring bold,
Prompt and assured as one who never fail'd.

The place he took, and captive made the king,
And gave the Island o'er to other sway,
And folded there awhile his soaring wing,
And ready made to ope his bridal day.

In Cyprus' ancient Isle did Richard wed,
Where spreading vines their purple clusters show,
And high in air Olympus lifts its head,
With Aphrodite's Temple 'mid its snow.

In this, the beauteous Isle of olden love,
Where still as Presence felt, though all unseen,
The Goddess in the sighing breeze did move,
And empire held as Beauty's radiant queen;

Where still the dreamy air her breath indrew,
Ambrosial e'er with every fragrant flower,
And o'er the place a mystic sweetness threw,
And Time was evermore the golden hour.

E'en here, where myrtles clothe the mountain side,
And flowery fields a paradise do make,
And rippling rills from craggy gorges glide,
And with sweet sound the feather'd choir awake,—

Here in this fair and all-enchanted spot
Did Richard blushing Berengaria wed ;
E'en here for good or ill they join'd their lot,
For thus the heavenly Scroll in faith they read :

For good or ill he join'd her to his soul
With links of gold Love girt the cestus round,
And blent their life in one harmonious whole,
And spread the inner Heavens o'er all the ground.

But sounds the trumpet loud athwart the sea,
From Akka came on Southern breeze the call,
And summon'd Richard, where upon the lea
Held Saladin proud Chivalry in thrall.

So from the beauteous Isle he wingèd flew,
And press'd his sails in haste to reach the place;
His glowing ardour shared the warrior crew,
As shone the light of Battle on his face.

To Akka came the Lion-hearted chief,
And swiftly changed the fortunes of the hour ;
Brought e'en his very presence sure relief,
Though fever through his veins its death did pour.

Along the trenches there on litter borne,
With look and tone that all the hero show'd,
Their ill success he bade them no more mourn,
And open'd once again high Glory's road.

For two dread years the siege had ebb'd and flow'd.
While Eastern prowess kept the West at bay ;
In nine stern fights, with sharp, unbending goad,
Had Selaheddin block'd the gory way.

But Richard came, and e'en, as one afore,
The gallant foe he conquer'd as he saw ;
And deathless is his name on Akka's shore,—
There weak and pale, yet giving battle's law.

But not at Akka only did he shine
Or spread the growing terror of his name,
At Jaffa soon doth Saladin decline,
As stubble falls before the rushing flame.

Twice from his rival's hold the place he tore,
Where pilgrims first do greet the " Pleasant Land,"
Twice on the foe did flaming vengeance pour
In mighty ire, hurl'd forth from Richard's hand.

With valour high he glow'd in Battle's field,
And cow'd the Arab 'fore his gleaming blade ;
He got him there what fame stern war could yield,
And so with Saladin a truce he made ;

A truce he made, and for the West he sail'd,
First sending on his bride with ample guard ;
The West he sought, his soul from wrath anneal'd,
In hope to join her on Sicilia's sward.

But ere from this dear land he sail'd away,
Which long afore he'd sought in yearning love,
And found again the world of common day
Where restless men in arid wastes do rove,—

One central spot there is to Jaffa near,
To which fond memory clings with tenderest thought,
There would he drop Love's consecrated tear,
And meekly own that sinful man is nought ;—

E'en there, where Love Himself sweet offering made,
And life became to all the dying world,
Where Beauty pierced the veil of earthly shade,
While Hell's dark surging hosts afar He hurl'd :—

There sweetly came this Lion-hearted man,
And view'd the Holy Place with living fear,—
Felt he a gentler essence in him ran
As heavenly voices woke his inner ear ;—

There, 'neath the boundless vault of Syrian blue,
Upon the summit of a neighbouring hill,
Entranced he stood, and wistful glances threw,
Where wingèd Passion bore his striving will.

Athwart the severing gulf his spirit flew ;
Before the blessèd Cross he bent him low,
And to the glorious Presence inly drew,
And oped his heart to drink its living flow.

So strengthen'd in his soul by might divine,
Thus flowing out from Him our sins that bare,
The place he left, but kept the inward sign,
And sought again without to do and dare.

PART III.

But first where Berengaria went afore,
He now essay'd with vast desire to go ;
He sought with her again to tread the shore
Where Faro lately heard them murmuring low.

He sought, but could not reach his cherish'd aim,
For adverse Fortune bore him far away :
Dark Envy strove to hide his glorious name,
And bar him from the light that weaves the day.

So Storm arose and caught him on its wave,
And drove him from Sicilia's Isle afar,
And show'd the deeps of Ocean's whelming grave,
And furious mix'd the elemental war ;

And hurl'd him on wild Istria's savage shore,
And gave him to the foes who wish'd him dead ;
And left him there unconscious evermore
If e'er he raised again his kingly head.

And so ere yet it took a gentler mood,
And wooed with placid breast the timid sail,
Is Richard seized with dastard hands and rude,
And Anglia soon doth weep with bitter wail.

For Austria's cunning duke, as Leopold known.
Though none of lion's nobleness he had,
Did seize and bear him off to castle lone,—
Wife's brother he to Cyprus' captive sad.

To gloomy Tyernsteign's dismal shades afar
Low ruffians bore in haste dear England's king ;
And there, without th' amenities of war,
The soaring eagle caged, now clipt of wing.

But soon to one of wider realm he pass'd,
And in the Tyrol hidden was from sight ;
There Henry base with fetters held him fast,
With fetters held this high-soul'd king and knight.

'Mid Tyrol's wooded glens and rippling rills
The captive Richard mourn'd sweet freedom fled.
And yearning sought the Everlasting Hills,
And pray'd that God would take him from the dead.

And now it is that inward strength he found,
Subsisting still from off the Cross he saw
That morn he stood on Palestina's ground
And read with Faith's clear eye pale Suffering's law.

At hallow'd Christmas tide, come round once more,
The strength from Godhead sprung his soul did hold;
And soar'd he far away from Time's dark shore,
And walk'd where angels tread the streets of gold.

So hidden here he lived as one who dreams
And sees the pleasant light above his head,
Yet cannot intermingle with its streams,
Nor with its sweet and radiant beauty wed.

Here spent he tedious days and wakeful nights,
Here Hope did wrestle oft with dark Despair;
Yet in this vaulted room of broken lights
He solace found in tragic song and prayer.

With mystic songs of love and knightly deeds
He wooed the Muses of immortal wing,
And pluck'd life's fragrant flowers and left its weeds.
And found in realm of mind he still was king.

And now upon a blithesome eve of spring,
When 'gins the turtle's throat to swell with song,
And children's voices in the twilight ring,
And lovers all the budding hedgerows throng;

Just as the sun was sinking in the West,
With melting glories all around him spread,
And balmy airs lull'd all the sense to rest,
And was his soul with tender memories fed;

Came on the evening breeze to Richard's ear
A sweet and plaintive strain from voice well known
A strain that sung how nought like love is dear.
How nought like *it* is fraught with Music's tone.

Struck on the captive's soul the thrilling lay
As look'd he from that guarded window there :
Caught he the budding hope of coming day,
As clomb that song the golden heights of prayer.

Not softest note of great Apollo's lute
Commingling with the sweet Pierian springs,
Nor tenderest note of gentliest breathing flute.
Is like to him who thus to Richard sings :—

   " O Richard, thou my glorious king,
     Great chief of war, high knight of love.
     Why foldest thou thine eagle wing,
     Or hast thou flown to realms above ?

   " O Richard, thou the Lion-king,
     Why hidest thou from love afar?
     Long have I sought to hear thee sing
     The lofty songs of love and war.

" O Richard, thou great Anglia's king,
   The people mourn thine absent face,
And to thy kingly soul do cling,
   And call thee from thy hiding place.

" O Richard, thou high knight of love,
   Pale Berengaria mourns thee fled,
Oh, weeps she lone in cypress grove,
   And murmurs low, 'not dead—not dead.'

" O Richard, thou my mighty lord,
   Great king among the kings of earth,
Oh, speak again the princely word,—
   Why should I die with famine's dearth?

" O Richard, O my glorious king,
   Great chief of war, high knight of love,
Pines all my soul to hear thee sing,
   To hear thee sing and no more rove."

Thus sung in plaintive strain the minstrel there,
And hallow'd all the place with lyric sound;
And knew the king by voice and accent rare,
'Twas Blondel's presence in the air he found.

And so as pray'd and moved by loving will,
The king well skill'd to frame the poet's lay,
With antiphonal song did Zephyr fill
Ere yet in coming night she died away.

" O Blondel, thou my minstrel dear,
　With voice attuned to love and war,
　Let not thy song e'er droop in fear ;
　But climb where gleams the Evening Star ;

" Where calmly shines the Star of Eve,
　In boundless deeps of space afar,
　And sweetly sings, look up, believe,
　There lift the song of love and war.

" There lift thy song, O minstrel dear,
　For lyric life is only there ;
　There doth it soar from year to year,
　And taste the sweets of praise and prayer.

" Where shines the Star of Eve ascend,
　With gushing joy the are attain,
　For doth it wings to morning lend,
　And leads the Sun along the plain.

" The Star of Eve, I love it well,
　Here captive kept from light of day ;
　Dear minstrel, cease dim sorrow's knell,
　The Star is Morn,—we'll hence away.

" The Star of Morn it hath become,
　My kingdom is mine own again ;
　To song and war, to wife and home,
　Go, say I come with heavenly gain."

Thus sung the king with manly voice and sweet,
As one that higher life hath found he sung ;
And Blondel bore the strain with striving feet
Where Anglia wept afar with anguish wrung.

And as it told where Richard lay immured,
What time high Easter's festival came round,
Some respite from his weightier grief endured
At Hageneau's council board it quickly found.

There came the king on Resurrection Morn,
And pled with flowing words great Freedom's law ;
From base sophistic art the lie was torn,
And quail'd they when his lofty truth they saw.

Refuses Song to tarry in that hall,
Or weariness assume with pedant lore,
Content to hear great Longchamp's mighty call,
Content to know the King to free he swore.

For Longchamp, Richard's stalwart regent known,
A priest who truth and right with strength upbore,
And held with potent hand the Lion's throne,
Till Faction from his hands the sceptre tore,

To Hageneau now had come with strenuous will,
Resolved his noble king should see the day,
And lift again his head from Fortune's ill,
And shed o'er Anglia's Isle his sunny ray.

RICHARD CŒUR DE LION.

So Longchamp there hard stipulation made
(For did the Teuton's greed compel his hand),
A kingdom's mighty ransom should be paid
Ere Richard yet should see his native land.

A hundred thousand marks the Teuton said,
(And Song doth weep to sing how mean is man,)
No guerdon less may free that Lion-head ;
And so the compact stood, for so it ran.

Not yet howe'er did Richard see the sun,
Not yet drank he sweet Freedom's bracing air ;
Waits he that ransom paid ere triumph's won,
And so returns to that harsh dungeon there.

So Spring in Summer's ardent breast dissolved,
And Summer 'fore the queenly Autumn fled ;
Came Winter on, and still he's unabsolved,
Still is the thorny crown wove round his head.

At length howe'er dear Spring doth come again,
And in the breezy morn sweet birds do sing ;
Peeps budding Beauty forth on hill and plain,
Moves colour'd cloud on high with lighter wing.

And now, O Richard, thou my glorious king,
My Muse doth call thee from that dungeon lone ;
Come forth and thine own pulsing sweetness fling
Athwart the lyre that sings anew thy throne.

And came great Richard forth, majestic, strong,
And on his brow a calmer beauty shone,
And facile chief he walk'd the kings among,
And show'd the inner conquests he had won.

Saw beauteous Rhine a brilliant pageant glide,
When Richard rode adown it to the sea,
And laugh'd a sunny laugh from side to side,
And spread the rapture far athwart the lea ;

And bore the gladness, too, along its stream,
And mix'd it soon with Ocean's bounding wave ;
Caught, too, its purple banks the waking dream,
As their deep base that joyous stream did lave.

But deeper is the joy athwart the sea,
The joy that fills a yearning Island there,
Where Freedom evermore doth make the free
Whose souls are pure and strong to act and dare.

In Anglia, Joy a river strong doth flow,
From place to place a torrent full it sweeps,
And onward as it moves doth swell and grow,
Awaiting one who's coming o'er the deeps.

And Joy once more did greet the Lion King,
Come back unto his own as from the dead,
And through the land loud pæans did it sing,
That Anglia's gloomy night at length had fled.

Come back, come back, King Richard is to-day,
And deepening plaudits fill the rapturous air;
And all along the gleaming watery way
Th' exultant Thames doth shout with jocund cheer.

Come back is he the Lion-heart again,
And sweeter, nobler, kinglier than afore;
And Joy doth sing in loud and long retrain,
"God save the King, God save him evermore."

And one there is to whom he's more than King,
Whose breast is heaved with e'en a deeper joy;
Soars she anew on Love's ecstatic wing,
And heavenliest bliss doth taste without alloy.

Dear dual life in one again to-day,
One sweetest music richer than before,
One soul upclimbing now the starry way,
One rapture they henceforth and evermore.

Eye greeteth eye with soft and sunny light,
Soul floweth unto soul in rapt embrace,
And hovering angels thrill to note the sight
They twain thus shedding glory on the Race.

But how may Song the heights of Love ascend,
Or show by sound the nature of the soul?
How sing the mighty spiral it doth wend,
In boundless orbit spurning all control?

The dazzling heights of Love the Muse doth quit,
The infinite of soul she leaves unsung,
Content at foot of Love for aye to sit,
Content if one sweet note the lyre hath flung.

One only strain she waiteth yet to sing,
One joy still climbeth up the sounding dome,
One yearning note still lingers on the string,
Which sung with folded wing she hieth home.

Late wore the Lion King a thorny crown,
And Anguish sat incarnate on his brow ;
Late gloomèd all the heavens with angry frown,
And nought saw he but chilling frost I trow.

But now the heavens have wheel'd their mighty frame,
And calm and clear is all the azure deep,
And he late hid now climbs the steeps of fame,
And soon, base traitors, shall ye quail and weep.

For Richard's star doth keep the zenith now,
And Anglia crowns again his kingly head ;
A second time she decks his noble brow,
A second time the king and kingdom wed.

For not his treacherous brother's cunning art
Can turn the People's love another way :
Chose they before, and still do keep their part,
And hail again with joy the bridal day.

So Anglia crowns again her king to-day,
And yields the splendid homage of her love,
What time sweet Easter beams with golden ray,
And Christ doth rise for aye in Heaven above.

And crown'd he rightly is, great king of men,
And for his truth and love he reigneth still,
The Lion now as Lion-hearted then,
Old England's brightest page he e'er shall fill.

The chief amongst her noblest sons he stands,
High knight of puissant Love, great king of War ;
And fragrant is his name in all the lands,
Where Venus softly breathes, or thunders Thor.

THE LADY GODIVA.

TIME was when knightly virtues clothed the soul,
And strove the sense to clear and raise the blood,
From darken'd eyes all cloud and mist to roll,
And bind the sever'd Race in brotherhood.

Time was when woman answer'd to the mood
And deck'd her glorious form with golden light,
When mercy in her sought the lone and rude,
And beat her pulse alone for holy right.

Time was when mailèd knight and gentle dame
Sweet compact form'd the sad with love to heal,
And found in storied page a cherish'd name,
And had no thought that left the common weal.

In such a time, eight hundred years ago,
When feudal bonds the State did hold as one,
When England's sky with deeper blue did flow,
And through the land did run a sweeter tone ;

THE LADY GODIVA.

At such a time, in one dark spot alone,
A brutal man and mean, miscall'd an earl,
Did cause the cumber'd widow's heart to groan,
Her madden'd brain with giddiness to whirl ;

For as tradition says, this mighty lord
A grievous tax imposed where none should fall,
And so unsheath'd a grim barbaric sword,
Which justice scorn'd in proud contempt of all.

In Mercia's woodland tract this low-brow'd churl,
Of stalwart limb, but mean and narrow soul,
Through some mad freak of nature found an earl,
His sordid chests to fill did fix the toll.

In that same place where now in dingy room
The pale and weary craftsman plies his toil,
And sounds all day the dismal noise of loom,
There smote this earl the loud-complaining soil.

With hawk and hound, fit symbols of his life,
He strode the fields as though they were his own,
While mourn'd at home his lone and grieving wife,
And all around the heavens did darkly frown :

For heard the listening heavens the people's moan,
And saw their watchful eye that lordling there,
And drew as golden mists the tears there sown,
And turn'd the weeping into radiant prayer:

And when on wearied eyes deep sleep did fall,
And vanish'd was the world in stilly night,
A voice sent forth with music in its call
Where rapt Godiva walk'd in realms of light.

In some bright angel sphere to her best known
She soar'd entranced this hallow'd summer night,
Intent to turn aside her people's moan,
And clothe them once again in festal white.

In vain she'd sought through many a striving hour
The word to break which stole the people's bread;
His freezing brow did but the darker lower,
While sternlier to his will the tax he wed.

So failing thus the tyrant's mood to change,
Though long she strove with words of pleading love,
Her soul unconscious took a wider range,
And rose in mystic dream her griefs above,

And found in spacious justice-halls on high,
Where Truth presides in flowing robes of light,
An answer to her love that clear'd her sky,
And roll'd away the shadows of her night.

For rising through her love to this high place,
As thither drawn by flaming spirits there,
Her people's joy she read in every face,
And eke that joy to reach, what she must dare !

For here, where Law doth find its hidden fount,
And Cause its primal motion takes unseen,
Is shown her rapt and calm on Vision's Mount
By subtle pulsings of the vital sheen,

How that to change the will which famine bred,
And stripp'd their scanty vestments from the poor,
Herself veil'd only with what lent her head,
On palfrey white should ride from door to door.

Godiva from the lofty vision woke at dawn,
And surged the swelling ocean through her soul ;
She thought and struggled long as one forlorn,
But will'd in love to reach the lofty goal.

As radiant morn, with fleecy glory crown'd,
Supplants with easy grace a weeping night,
So on her brow a beauteous light is found,
As moves she victor in the arduous fight.

Once more the stolid earl she met alone,
And urged the suit which sought the people's weal.
But now with deeper ardour in the tone,
As one high deed of love about to seal.

He heard her much as he had done before,
Or may be e'en in darker mood of soul ;
For now, as if he'd bar for aye the door
Of those sweet lips ere they the guerdon stole.

He shamele s tied the brutal tax anew,
And bound it to her pure and tender form,
And in her blushing face the scorn he threw,
That if the commonwealth she would reform,

She should ride naked through the busy town,
What time the sun his zenith should attain,
And get, if so she pleased, a vast renown,
Dreaming his tax to save by her disdain.

So said, he pass'd from audience to the field,
To sport him with his dogs as was his wont,
And little deem'd that love her form could shield,
And e'en as blessed thing the trial count.

But love we know had conquer'd in her breast :
She only saw wan children cry for bread,
She only thought to give their mothers rest,
And lift again to light the weary head.

So came this peerless lady forth at noon,
Transfigured with the shining of her love :
And as in summer night doth ride the moon,
With sweet and calm effulgence deck'd above.

So rode Godiva in the Heavens this day,
The deep blue azure of her radiant soul,
While Chastity in every house her way
Did ope as forth she ambled to the goal.

Pure chastity, I say, each house did grace,
As rode this glorious woman on her way,
While holy Love's Evangel lit her face,
And lent all needful veil before high day.

She pass'd, a beauteous vision all unseen,
With Nature gently lull'd to pleasant sleep;
Sweet dreams alone did stir the golden sheen,
Low murmurs of the dove awoke the deep:

She pass'd in grace of love along the line,—
One traitor only sought to bar her way;
He madly sought, but gave no open sign,
For instant blindness smote the guilty ray

She pass'd—in grace of love she bore her on,
Till show'd the hawthorn with its living green.—
And sweetest victory she nobly won,—
And shall she live for aye, high Beauty's queen.

F

BANBURY CROSS.

WHEN Stephen of the Norman line
The crown attain'd in oblique way,
And found its pressure not benign,
And often wish'd he'd stopp'd away,—

For that the land was up in arms,
And faction rent the State in two,
And everywhere were sown alarms,
While doubtful voices wildly grew,—

When up and down the groaning sphere
The tramp of hoofs did shake the air,
And mailèd knights with sword and spear
Did leave at home their ladies fair,

And sallied forth in knightly mood
High battle's solemn wage to try,
And take the evil or the good
As should be shown in destiny,—

In such a time, when things were loose
And much disjointed from their frame,
And not a man who own'd a goose
Could be quite sure to eat the same,—

In such a time it came to pass,
As fond tradition long hath said,
A certain man did love a lass,
And loving, all but lost his head.

Hereby, howe'er, a tale hath hung,
The which to tell I yield my lay,
And move the lyric spheres among,
And hope to take you on my way.

So be it known thus stood the case,
Which now to History's eye I bring
(I pray that Muse she won't grimace
If I should somewhat flag on wing):

Two rival Houses had a feud,
Though what about I cannot say;
Suffice it, that both fierce and rude
They champ'd the bit the livelong day.

Like fiery steeds they champ'd the bit,
Impatient for the field of Mars,—
Came in grim war—went out sweet wit,
And nought was heard but clashing jars.

Their names, though famous in their time,
Are drownèd in dark Lethe's lake ;
They rest in its abysmal slime,—
There let them sleep, nor e'er awake.

But as a poet free, who makes
Whate'er his fancy wills to find,
And with his song the welkin wakes,
I name them as I feel inclined :

So one the Norman House I name,
Bright blue blood flowing in its vein,
Which lately with the Conqueror came,
And rooted was beneath his reign :

The rival House I Saxon call,
Whose blood was of a thicker kind ;
This by the first was held in thrall,
And hence no doubt this storm of wind.

The Norman House, tradition tells,
With son and daughter radiant shone,
And with loquacious fondness dwells
Upon their loftiness of tone.

The Saxon House, as fame hath said,
A son alone as wealth did own,
In whom its sole surviving head
All future joy and hope were sown.

Where Banbury's pleasant town doth rise,
Outlooking on the fertile West,
With Cross uprising to the skies,
And cakes and ale the very best,

In this fair town, to Oxon near,
These famous Houses had their seat,
Here strove and fought from year to year,
And clutch'd the chaff and dropp'd the wheat.

The feud it burn'd for many a day,
And blazing lit the country side ;
Yet not without a calmer ray
Which did into these Houses glide :

A beam it was from Cupid's bow,
Much like an arrow in its form,
All keen and bright, and so and so,
And soon it raised a pleasant storm.

For though the Sires were very stern,
And daggers shot from glancing eyes,
Two lovers met by brook and fern,
And pledged their troth afore the skies :

For Cupid's shaft had found its aim,
Transpiercing through both flesh and bone,
And lit an inward burning flame,
Low breathing in an undertone.

So, though the feud was long and deep,
Electric Love was first a-field ;
Loved he before the dawn of sleep,
And sceptre vast did proudly wield.

So Saxon thane met Norman lass,
Close drawn by Love's attraction sweet ;
They met and look'd in Cupid's glass,
And vow'd they ne'er would beat retreat.

But as their love grew thick and fast,
And effloresced in walk and talk,
There cross'd them one, who stood aghast,
And swore their pleasant dreams to baulk.

The Norman brother he of her
Who leant the Saxon's arm upon,—
And mighty bother did he stir,
As seeing what his eyes look'd on.

With prelude none he fiercely spoke,
The lightning glancing in his eye ;
While all the Norman in him woke,
This vision strange to see go by :

"A Saxon churl," quoth he, in haste,
"Hath nought to do with Norman blood ;
We meet to-night athwart the waste
To try the evil and the good."

Thus having said, he turn'd on heel,
And left the lovers to their fate ;
The girl in tears, the man all steel,
And quick with sword to quench the hate.

And now in Passion's lofty speech
Their life for aye to each they gave,
And linger'd till the sun did reach
The broad Atlantic's gleaming wave :

The sun in crimson light went down,
And fair the autumn woods were seen,
In all the dome you saw no frown
Of cloud or mist to dim the scene.

A moment more, and clomb the arc
A moon which shone with brilliant ray ;
Yet was the night with horror dark,
Where haste the foemen on their way.

They cross the waste, they near the wood,
And seek its shade their deed to hide :
For needs their soul some mantling hood,
Thus ranged in combat side by side :

No word is spoke, a look is given,
And then the clash of swords is heard,
And soon the sound of armour riven,
And blood down-trickling on the sward :

A moment more, and prostrate seen
The Saxon thane is on the ground,
With little hope to rise, I ween,
And join again stern battle's sound.

A deadly thrust has laid him there,
And fast the crimson tide doth flow ;
But rises near the voice of prayer
From one that's pallid as the snow.

And as the life doth ebb and fail,
Another life its tide doth pour,
And with Love's might doth countervail
In part to close Death's open door.

Pale, bleeding from a deadly wound,
The thane is borne from off the field ;
His blood down-streaming on the ground—
His passion gone—his hate anneal'd.

Straight to his father's house he's borne,
And placed, a dying man, a-bed ;
All pale his face, with anguish torn,
And hanging low his drooping head.

The Saxon lay a-bleeding there,—
The maiden hasten'd to a cave
Where dwelt a lonely man of prayer,
And sought that failing life to save.

With wingèd steps she reach'd the place,
Near by the dread and cruel field,
In hope to read upon his face
What mighty destiny should yield.

With few quick words she told her tale,
And bathed it with her flowing tears ;
The hermit smooth'd her forehead pale,
And bid her hold her gloomy fears.

" A sovereign balm," quoth he, " I tell,
Thou'lt lift again his drooping head ;
My word observe, and keep it well,
And with high manna thou'lt be fed.

"In Banbury's midst a Cross doth rise,
Deep symbol of Eternal Love;
It calmly seeks the archèd skies,
And breathes a Name their are above.

" And wondrous potence hath it found,
As join'd to Him who bless'd its form,
Weak souls to raise above the ground,
And heal their wounds and hush their storm.

" So then, when silent is the night,
And sinks the World in sleep profound,
Go thou, with love and meekness dight,
And music thrilling all the ground :

"On palfrey white with girded vest
And silvery sounds of tinkling bell,
When sinks the sun below the west
Ride forth in faith thy beads to tell.

"Thrice round the sacred Cross proceed,
With prayer and praise and deathless love,
On three successive nights decreed,
And thou'lt prevail in Courts above."

As one late dead, but raised again,
The maiden heard this saintly man,
And sung her soul in long refrain
A low melodious orison.

As seeks the knight the tardy morn
When sleeps the battle on the plain,
So is the maid with vigils worn
Till she her heavenly guerdon gain.

At length the car of night wheel'd round,
And brought the high and festal hour,
When as the queen of love she's found,
With joy triumphant evermore.

The long'd-for night at last was come,
And beauteous was the face it wore,—
Fair shone the moon in Heaven's blue dome,
As left the maid her father's door.

On palfrey white rode forth she well,
In solemn silence of the night,
With silvery sounds of tinkling bell,
Soft blending with the mellow light.

Thrice round the Cross she calmly rode,
And thought of Him who bless'd its form,
And from her soul was ta'en the load
Which darkly heaved her breast with storm

On three successive nights she came
With silvery sounds of tinkling bell,—
With holy love's ascending flame
Thrice round the Cross she rode right well:

Thrice round the sacred Cross she rode
On three successive nights decreed,
With music all along the road,
Entrancing stream, and copse, and mead.

And now her prayer high potence had,
And chased grim Death who linger'd near;
Her lover once more raised his head,
And walk'd abroad with vision clear.

From deadly wound and fever'd blood
The Saxon, strange to tell, rose up;
And knew the evil and the good,
For drank he deep life's bitter cup.

Oh, wondrous is the power of prayer!
Oh, beauteous is the might of love!
Around the Cross they triumph'd there,
While pæans sang the Heavens above.

And not the Heavens alone did sing,—
The rival Houses now were one;
The lovers soar'd on higher wing,
And soon were led to Hymen's throne.

EDITHA:

A LEGEND OF TARIFA.

PART I.

WHERE Cornwall's high and craggy line
Looks on the broad Atlantic wave,
And shows to home-sick souls a sign
That dewy eyes with joy doth lave ;

What time returning from afar
The soldier scans his native soil,
And rest would have from storm of war
And all his weary travel-toil :

Where high projects that point of land
Which first salutes his wistful view,
And lone in air, above the strand,
Her snowy wings doth flap the mew:

There, in a rocky nook withdrawn,
An ancient castle grimly frown'd,
Uprear'd in Knighthood's martial dawn,
With loop'd and lofty turrets crown'd :

There dwelt a knight, Sir Geoffrey known,
With cousin Editha his ward;
In that stern castle, all alone,
These two did vigil keep and guard.

The knight a man of stalwart frame,
Broad in the chest and strong of arm.
From warlike ancestors he came,
And knew nor fear nor dim alarm.

The maid a flower not fully blown,
Though lately won by Cupid's art,—
A flower some eighteen summers sown,
With gentle tumult at the heart.

Of slender form and fair in hue,
And wavy locks of flowing gold,
And eyes that caught the heavenly blue,
And dainty feet that spurn'd the mould.

The knight himself had felt her ray,
And sunn'd his soul beneath her smile,
But found she'd ta'en another way
With one she'd met—from him a mile.

One mile away on headland high
Sir Alured soar'd in battled hall,
And with the hawks possess'd the sky,
And broke the sea with rocky wall.

And from his eyrie in mid air
He'd swoop'd as eagle on the plain,
And seized as prey sweet Edith there,
And ne'er would let her go again.

And now as opes my gentle lay
He to the castle wings his flight,
For dawn has brought his marriage-day,
And all his sky is filled with light.

Sounds sweet and clear the village chime,
The banquet waits with flowers and fruit,—
The lovers pluck the golden time,
And life renew at Eden's root.

One face was pallid at the board,
And challenged, smiled a sickly smile ;
One heart was piercèd with a sword,
And chid the nearness of that mile.

The lives are join'd, the stream is one,
And so doth flow for many a day,
When broken is the unison,
And take the streams a sever'd way.

From southern Spain report has come
How that the sword doth naked gleam,—
And thither knightly men do roam
In strength to breast war's torrent-stream.

The gallant Prince, third Edward's son,
Who now had broke the spears of France
(As brave a man as sun shone on),
Will prove the might of Spanish lance.

And so where fought high Transtamare,
With question of disputed right,
And battle raged both far and near
Don Pedro's lines to chase in flight,

There fought the Prince on Pedro's side,
As first in blood and tenure found;
There did he charge and swiftly ride,
And smite his foe at trumpet's sound.

So there Sir Alured hastes to stand
And join the battle's surging wave,
Where high Tarifa spurns the strand,
And in the clouds her head doth lave.

So pass'd he to this foreign shore,
While Edith pined and droop'd at home;
And seem'd it he no longer wore
The clearness of the azure dome.

A gay and gallant cavalier,
He'd weary grown of home's still life,
And so is at Tarifa here,
And little mindful of his wife.

A courtly and a handsome man,
With passion stirring all the blood;
From flower to flower he gaily ran,
And loved at large the sisterhood.

So here in Spain from home afar
He throweth loose sweet Fancy's rein,
And in the interludes of war
Wakes with wild love the sleeping plain.

And so his wife is all forgot ;
And weary months she weeps alone,
And thinks how dark and sore her lot
That he so soon should change his tone.

So waiting long, but hearing nought,
She sent Sir Geoffrey to the place,
To search the cause the change that wrought,
And chase the pallor from her face.

Yet this dear guerdon did he crave,
That if Sir Alured should be dead,
She'd sweetly take the love he gave
And bid him lift his drooping head.

So Geoffrey touch'd the coast of Spain,
And with Sir Alured fought right well,
Yet no fond message came again,
No tidings of him did he tell.

I

Moon follow'd moon in tardy round,
Each sicklier than the one before,
Yet not a word from Spanish ground,
No welcome sound of cheery oar.

And now upon a stormy night,
When sere and brown was Autumn's leaf,
And blotted was all glimpse of light,
And loudly roar'd the sea beneath ;

And flew the petrel o'er the deep,
Nor rest could find upon the shore,
While 'woke the winds from fitful sleep
And drove the crested waves afore;

When darkest was this wailing night
Pale Edith trod the banquet floor,
And all at once is smote with fright,
With fright as from a creaking door.

Upon the wall before her hung
A coat of mail Sir Alured wore,
What time in hall the minstrels sung
And full the cup of joy flow'd o'er.

With weird and low metallic clang
The armour-joints together close,
A mournful dirge within her sang,
And all her blood it straightway froze.

It could not be the noise of wind,
For it had lull'd some rest to take;
It was some hidden force of mind
That shook her soul—now ruffled lake.

Oh wondrous are the links of mind,
Far reaching from the burning throne,
Each link a thought that shames the wind
When swift it flies from zone to zone.

Some thought it was that shook the mail,
Not wind or clumsy wire, I ween,—
Some thought from watching spirit pale
Who long that drooping wife had seen,

And call'd her thus to one in Spain,
And show'd him in great peril there,
And bade her haste athwart the main
And save him by her love and prayer.

Thus Edith read the mystic sound;
With trusty squire she cross'd the sea,
And lit her foot on Spanish ground,
Sweet land of dream and minstrelsy.

By vision clear of deep-eyed love
She found the camp where Alured fought.
And there a gallant page she strove,
And battle's might with him she sought.

As page she join'd him all unknown,
For battle clothèd all her brow;
And he an alter'd man had grown;
And hid she deep her smother'd woe.

So then at eve the Camp she found,
With battle waiting for the sun,—
A snowy field of tented ground,
Where to and fro swift heralds run.

Came now at length the blushing morn,
With sighings of the startled air,
And trembled prickly briar and thorn
As sounded shrill the trumpets' blare.

The serried lines in thunder close,
Bright lances shiver in the shock,
Swift riders fell and never rose,
While some were planted as the rock.

Where deepest flow'd the crimson tide,
Where fiercest surged stern battle's wave,
There Alured rode with page at side
And with his lance ope'd many a grave.

But one he met, a knight of Spain,
High skill'd to wed with battle's hour,
Who never charged but ope'd a lane,
And fell'd his foes as grass the mower.

Thus swept Diego o'er the plain,
With light'ning speed he clear'd his way:
Sat on his brow a proud disdain
As mix'd he in the stern affray.

So chanced it as he wingèd flew
With lance in rest some foe to seek,
Sir Ahmed from his horse he threw
In tug of war as Greek meets Greek.

And now as on the plain he lay,
The final blow about to fall,
His page held back the twilight grey
And interposed a sheltering wall.

Between him and the Spanish knight
The gallant page rush'd boldly in,
And had the blow, and sunk in night,
And heard no more the battle's din.

And now the life-blood trickling fast
The faithful page had rested there,
And fitful dream had found the past,
And closed his eyes to all things here,

But that the knight with pity flow'd
As caught his eye the bleeding boy;
So with him to his tent he rode,
And nursed him there with noble joy.

With tender care this knightly man,
Whose soul was gentle as the dove,
Stripp'd from his frame all stiff and wan
The chainèd coat his lance had rove,

And calling leeches to his aid,
As search'd they close the reeking wound,
He found the seeming page was maid,
And wonder'd much at what he found.

So now to quiet Convent near
The Don Diego bore the page,
Where battle sounds not on the ear,
But life is still from age to age.

PART II.

In Autumn's sweet and trancing hour,
When sigh the woods with pleasing dream,
And gentlier song the birds do pour,
And mellow lights shade-soften'd gleam:

And yearns the soul in mystic thought
The arc to climb and ope the door
Whence all this loveliness is wrought,
And Heaven's high King to come before:

To come before Him radiant there
With beauty and with glory dight,
To come and yield the heart in prayer
And drink with joy His higher light.

E'en now as wings this golden hour,
And holy seems this Earth again,
There soundeth from the Convent tower
A chime all sweet with love's refrain.

It is the Convent call to prayer,
It is low music warbling there,
It is the soul upon the air,
And Angels rapt with listening ear.

Woke Edith with the soothing sound
From fever'd sleep and troubled dream,
And all about her heart it wound,
And dear as wedded love did seem.

And lo, as beam'd again her eye
With flowing light from life resown,
She saw the Don her couch anigh,
And heard and kept his knightly tone.

In high discourse their voices blent,
With wingèd thoughts their spirits soar,
Beyond the dome their message went,
Nor stay'd till at th' Eternal door.

Anon of fickle spouse she spoke,
He listening to her tragic tale,
And all the knight within him woke
And swell'd to storm as doth the gale.

Thus many days their circuit run,
And oft they met in friendly talk,
Conversing of the absent one,
And questioning much where he might walk.

So when sweet health came back once more
And rounded was her fallen cheek,
They two did quit the Spanish shore
That false and absent one to seek.

For was he not in Spanish bound,
Nor could his travels there be known ;
So haste they to that other ground
Where Edith first her tears had sown.

In gallant barque they sail'd the sea,
That Spanish knight and Edith fair,
And drank its stately melody
And mingled in its ceaseless prayer.

The blithe and dancing Spring had come
Since Edith found that convent shade,
Yet all its voice to her was dumb
And but a mournful music made.

So fitted more her deeper mood
The deep broad sea with mighty roar,
With hungry soul she took the food
And glanced behind but look'd before.

To things before her vision flew,
And strength arose with every wave,
From tiny mustard seed it grew,
To death succumb'd—then left the grave.

And he who held and cheer'd her way,
And show'd how pure is knighthood's life,
Did chase the night with struggling day,
While honour'd he the name of wife.

So thus they dwelt in golden spheres
As swept the barque athwart the sea,
They saw afar th' Eternal years,
And triumph'd in their harmony.

But now as rose the Cornish coast
Coterminous with the archèd sky,
To him who clomb the towering mast
And shouted loud of land the cry;

A tempest gather'd o'er the deep,
With silent step it stealthy came,
Yet soon shook off its seeming sleep,
And swept in fury as the flame.

From stem to stern the wind did sweep,
Anon 'midships athwart it went;
Groan loud the masts, the timbers creak,
And soon the 'leaguer'd hull is rent.

Broke up the barque with wailing cry,
Though lower'd first the boats in awe;
In these afore the storm they fly,
And wildly rush from Ocean's jaw.

With life scarce pluck'd from out the deep,
That strove with vast Titanic power,
They're borne to land with 'whelming sweep,
And stricken press the sounding shore.

And chanced it that the wreck was near
The towering cliff to Edith known,
And thither in the evening drear
They bent their steps to Ocean's moan.

Along the line of coast they trod
As sickly gleam'd the struggling moon,
Their hearts all silent as the sod,
As wrapp'd in that now coming soon.

With painful steps and slow they moved,
The knight upholding with his arm,
While e'er with gentle looks he soothed
Her soul, whose instinct saw the harm:

The cruel harm, the cruel harm,
Which then enacting was anigh,
With no remorse and no alarm,
No smothered tear or stifled sigh.

Anon the fatal spot is seen.
Behold, the lofty crag is there;
High in the air with nought of screen,
And hallow'd not with voice of prayer.

There frowns the crag above the hills,
And there Sir Alured's castle stands;
And down the crag stream pleasant rills,
And music pour athwart the lands.

But what is passing there to-night?
What mean those lights? is Edith's thought.
Why is the place with radiance dight?
What is there said, and what is wrought?

With gloomy dread they seek the height,
Within the hall pale Edith stood;
A moment, and grew dim her sight,
And anguish pour'd its bitter flood.

An ample curtain drap'd the door,
The inner door where stood she there;
The veil she drew, and saw on floor
A splendid feast unmix'd with prayer.

A gorgeous marriage feast she saw,
With flowers and song, and flowing wine;
And in the night-air chill and raw,
Went forth aghast and gave no sign.

Into the dark, dark night she came,
Back to the weird and howling wind;
With pallid brow and heart aflame,
And madness wrecking all the mind.

Down to the roaring sea they came,
And answer'd deep its plaintive wail;
They saw, but breathèd not his name,
And waited for to-morrow's sail.

In homely cot the night they spent,
And wistful sought the tardy dawn,
And with it on the beach they went,
A ship to seek being thither drawn.

And low as now they tarry there,
In anxious mood to quit the place,
A footstep sounded on the air,
And came anear a well-known face.

For Geoffrey sought the breezy morn
Which came upon that dismal night;
And Edith met he there forlorn,
And inly thrill'd he at the sight.

Aside they talk'd for many an hour,
While press'd he them his board to share ;
And Edith all her heart did pour,
And told why stood they waiting there.

He heard her tale—he mark'd her woe,
And once again her hand did seek ;
While reason'd he both to and fro,
And last did bend him at her feet.

But Edith gently bade him rise,
And said her husband was not dead ;
She said they'd meet in yonder skies,
And there in love eternal wed.

So parted they, nor met again,
Save in the awful World unseen ;
And with the Don she cross'd the main,
And shelter found where she had been.

Within the Convent's calm retreat
She sought her stricken soul to heal ;
Her sandals ta'en from off her feet,
She sought that cruel husband's weal.

Thus pass'd the golden hours away,
For golden they as crown'd with love ;
Till came again an Autumn day,
When Angels called her up above.

From Sorrow's lone and clouded night,
They called her bruisèd soul away,
To dwell where is the fount of light,
And rapturous pæans sing for aye.

Beside her couch Diego wept
With knightly and with holy tears;
While she as infant calmly slept,
And pass'd beyond the realm of fears.

And now within his soul he knew
What long high love had whisper'd there;
How round about his heart she grew,
And yet had vanish'd in the air.

As one whose life is rent in twain,
The knight a widow'd state doth feel;
With love's keen arrows inly slain,
He strove in vain—he could not heal.

So ere sweet Spring with balmy air
Had come again to vernal bowers,
He soar'd into the realm of prayer,
And knew no more Earth's clouded hours.

And Geoffrey, too, stay'd not behind,
For love had riven long his soul;
So pass'd he as on wings of wind,
To know on high the sever'd whole.

And now Sir Alured dwelt alone,
Alone, with Edith his no more ;
For hers is not a wifely tone
Who restless walks that silent floor.

So weary days do come and go,
And lone and wakeful nights remain ;
He walks the Earth a man of woe,
And soon a-hunting he is slain.

For on a day when Winter's near,
And light is grey and air is chill,
He's smitten in his hall with fear,
His spirit dies with boding ill.

With hunting spear and merry horn,
He cross'd in doubt his spacious floor ;
When lo ! he sees, all pale and worn,
Two haggard spectres at the door.

With heavy heart he rode a-field,
Nor skill'd to ride as heretofore ;
His drooping hand the rein did yield,
He saw no more that awful door.

MABEL:

A LEGEND OF OLD ST. PAUL'S.

WHEN bluff King Harry ruled the land
And England was a merrie place,
And Time all jovial dropp'd his sand,
And stalwart was the fighting race;

When fought our men with twanging bow
And slew their foes at point of lance,
And scorn'd them down in line to mow
With blustering guns like braggart France;

When noisy towns were few and small
And kept their place as towns should do,
And sought not to engulph us all
In one vast wilderness of woe;

When fair the azure dome was seen,
And smoke as yet was far away,
And came not near that peerless sheen,
And one could tell when day was day;

When looms that fill our ears with din
And break our men with servile toil
Had not yet trod the way of sin
Nor round us clung with snaky coil;

When there were fields where folks could walk
And, festal clad, make holiday,
And each could hear as each did talk,
And open was the King's highway;

When iron lines and 'lectric wires
Were firmly lock'd in teeming brains,
And men liked more tall village spires,
Nor wanted to be stunn'd with trains:

When Thought did muse in quiet hour,
And men of letters lit their lamp,
And London was not brimming o'er
With stuff as dreary as a swamp;

When struck the soul a fiery light,
And Wyat sung and Surrey fought,
And More Utopia dream'd at night,
And Cranmer at reforming wrought;

When old St. Paul's majestic stood
With ample space around its wall,
Where man sought man in brotherhood
And answer'd to his neighbour's call;

K

Then, in that pleasant olden time,
The story which I sing had place,
And bruited was through all the clime,
And doubtless had a living face.

A story done in flesh and blood,
And well deserving to be known,
Of maiden fair, and priest not good,
Arraign'd before King Harry's throne.

So now, good people, ope your ears,
And listen to my growing lay;
And take your fill of hopes and fears,
As hies the story on its way.

A maid there was as Mabel known,
Who fell in love, as maids will do,
And loved a man who served the Crown,
And proved the love in manner new.

Now Mabel was of comely form,
Where Beauty dwelt as in her home:
And here do lie the cloud and storm,
Which now will force my tale to roam.

So be it known, as on a day
She sought the shrine already sung,
There to confess in lowly way,
And mourn the sins which round her clung.

Dark looks he sent, dark things he thought,
E'en as she pray'd before him there ;
Nor with his tempting demon fought,
Then floating in the murky air.

And so as Mabel tearful sought
Absolving grace some sin to free,
His evil will he darkly wrought,
And penance gave as remedy.

The penance was at depth of night,
At depth of night within the shrine,
When gone is every sound and sight,
And life should be a solemn time.

But not alone his art he plied,
Which strove the maid to seize as prey ;
It sought her lover, too, to hide,
Where ne'er he'd see the light of day.

And this to compass, as he thought,
He wily compact made with one
Who with the Yeoman's guard had fought,
Wherein the absent lover shone.

A cunning covenant he made,
With priestly guerdon for the hire ;
Then pass'd they on to creep in shade,
And feed their souls with hellish fire.

At depth of night the maiden came,
Her penance in the shrine to do,
Where dimly burnt a taper's flame,
Nor saw the black impending woe.

She came, and by an altar stood,
In act to bend the knee in prayer;
When stealthy crept, with darksome hood,
The wicked priest long hiding there.

He madly thought the maid to hold,
And bend her to his evil mind;
But she with horror shunn'd the fold,
And swiftly rush'd, as doth the wind,

And found at hand an open door,
Which to the belfry-tower did bring:
With maddening fear at every pore
She flew—she flew on fiery wing;

And reach'd the floor where hung the ropes,
Which levers were to sound the chimes;
There kindled she her failing hopes
By striking loud the dying times.

The floor she reach'd, with him behind,
As struck the clock the midnight hour,
When forth she sent upon the wind
Another stroke from that high tower.

Adown the Eastern wind it crept,
And stirred the air in Windsor's glades;
And startled one who had not slept,
But paced his beat in silent shades.

And now as struck that novel sound,
Loud echoing in the stilly night,
The monks forsook the hallow'd ground
Where waited they the dawn of light.

From psalms and orisons they came
To seek the meaning of the knell;
When Mabel met them all aflame
Against that priest of purpose fell.

So to their friendly arms she ran,
And there breathed forth the prayer unsaid.
While shrunk away the guilty man,
With wrath impending o'er his head.

The dread night pass'd, and came the morn,
And Mabel rose from wakeful bed;
And burning, flew on wings of storm
On lover's breast to rest her head.

The priest, too, followed in her wake,
Intent to learn how sped his guile,
For would he not his prey forsake,
Nor turn aside his treacherous smile.

Meantime the man whom Mabel loved,
Whose arm she sought her life to guard,
She found from audience far removed,
A chainèd prisoner kept in ward.

For while as yet the dawn was young,
And strove the sun to ope his way,
A dastard lie from hell was flung,
With aim to blast his budding May.

For said the man the priest that join'd,
" I saw him sleep upon his watch ;"
And little dreamt the word he coin'd
Was death for him upon the latch.

" I saw him lock'd in sleep," he said,
" What time the midnight hour came round :
In heaviest sleep he droop'd his head ;
He saw no sight, he heard no sound."

Now death it is, by soldier's law,
To yield to sleep at sentry's post ;
And Death was near with open jaw,
And inly cried, "Give up the ghost."

But who shall shed life's crimson stream ?
And who shall join the gloomy shades ?
Is this, the prisoner asks, wild dream,
Or did I hear it in those glades ?

In presence of the Yeoman's king,
The dread tribunal held its seat ;
With oath he now the lie did fling,
And pour'd the chaff and hid the wheat.

" Upon his watch I saw him sleep,
At twelve at night," quoth he ; " the time
Strong Silence held him in the deep,
He saw no sight, he heard no chime."

Thus swore the churl the deadly lie,
And poured the chaff and kept the wheat,
Nor saw a witness in the sky,
That now drew near and told the cheat.

For loves the Sky what's true and pure,
And hateth all that makes a lie ;
And so now made it clear and sure,
That East to West did send a cry :

A cry at midnight hour did send,
A cry as of metallic sound,
Which in the stilly air did wend,
And woke the night for miles around.

And this was all the prisoner's plea,
This was his life when death drew near,—
That down the wind a sound did flee,
A sound which struck his listening ear,

At that same hour at dead of night,
When, as was sworn, he deeply slept,
And heard no sound, and saw no sight,
Nor felt the breeze that o'er him swept :

E'en now, in silence of the night,
Upon the air then whispering low,
If heard his wakeful ear aright,
There came with solemn step and slow,

A novel sound from some huge bell,
That gave a stroke unheard before,
And increase made to midnight's knell,
And startled e'en as thunder's roar.

He heard the knell, he mark'd the times,
His soul was calm, and quick his ear;
He said Saint Paul's struck thirteen chimes,
Nor more could say if present there.

But one is in this judgment hall,
Who well the wondrous secret knew ;
E'en she who woke that mighty call,
And for whose sake it wingèd flew.

So Mabel told her thrilling tale,
Before the King her grief she laid,
And show'd how rose that midnight wail,
And strengthened all her lover said.

Heard this sad tale King Henry there,--
With swelling ire he heard it told :
When sunk the priest with guilty fear,
And in that presence lifeless roll'd.

Doom'd, too, was he the lie that made,
He join'd the priest among the dead :
While sprung the lover from the shade,
And Mabel to Love's altar led.

II

CUM LYRÁ.

"JOY COMETH IN THE MORNING."

THE chalice fill with ruby wine,
For radiant is my soul to-day;
Gone is the gloom, nor left a sign,
Which long hath barr'd my gushing lay.

My chalice fill with sparkling wine,
For Joy doth build my sky to-day.
Henceforth the laurel wreath is mine
To crown at last my conquering way.

The chalice fill with gladdening wine,
For I must needs keep holiday;
Dear wife, I join my lips to thine,
And yield me to thy sunny ray.

My chalice fill with mellow wine,
And let me live the days of youth,
And taste again that happy time,
And dream its dreams and drink its truth.

The chalice fill with generous wine,
And bring once more my cunning lyre.
In bower of rose and eglantine
I'll wake again its slumbering fire.

My chalice fill with lordly wine,
For breaketh forth my soul in Song ;
I strike its chords, and touch the line
Which bears me up the Stars among.

"THE FLOWER FADETH."

Gone for ever—down Life's river
    Are the thoughts of yesterday :
Reach, Love, forth thy bow and quiver.
    Let me sport anew to-day.

Gone for ever—down Life's river
    Are the dreams of Early Youth :
Come, Love, come, immortal ever,
    Feed my soul with higher truth.

Gone for ever—down Life's river
    Are the joys I thought to keep :
Holy Love, desert me never,
    Leave me not alone to weep.

Gone for ever—down Life's river
    Are the budding hopes of Spring :
Mighty Love, thy hold ne'er sever,
    Bear me on thine Eagle-wing.

Gone for ever—down Life's river
     Are the friends of former years :
Faithful Love, thou'st fled not thither,
     Thou wilt dry my flowing tears.

Gone for ever—down Life's river
     Seems my soul in Sorrow's night :
Kingly Christ, that soul's endeavour,
     Thou art strength and life and light.

"WITH EAGLE'S WINGS."

SOARING ever up the Ether,
Wingèd mounts my soul to-day,
Longing much for calmer weather
In that lone and distant way.

Soaring ever through the Ether,
Ranges free my thought for aye,
Seeking light and strength to gather
In an everlasting day.

Soaring ever up the Ether,
Rises Hope on golden wings,
Leaving dark Despair beneath her,
While in pæans glad she sings.

Soaring ever through the Ether,
Rambles Joy in sportive play,
Crown'd with orange-bloom and heather,
Pouring forth a jocund lay.

E.

Soaring ever up the Ether,
Love ascends with beaming eye,
Streams a trail of glory 'neath her
As she climbs the upper sky.

Soaring ever on the Ether,
Faith doth dwell as in her home,
Shouts with trumpet come up hither,
Weary souls who weep alone.

"WHERE IT LISTETH."

WHERE it listeth gently breathes the wind,
Dimly stealing from some mystic cave ;
As it willeth softly flows the mind,
Pouring music from its dulcet wave.

Where it listeth freely blows the wind,
Roaming widely o'er the earth and sea ;
As it pleaseth acts at will the mind,
Sailing on the light with motion free.

Where it listeth wildly sighs the wind,
Telling deeply of some tragic ill ;
As it fainteth strongly cries the mind,
Moaning sadly from a darkened hill.

Where it listeth swiftly moves the wind,
Driving fiercely through a stormy sky ;
As it burneth wingèd flies the mind,
Grandly going forth in ecstasy.

Where it listeth darkly steals the wind,
Hiding closely where it wakes and sleeps ;
As it chooseth inly keeps the mind,
Calmly thinking wholly in the deeps.

Where it listeth ever roams the wind,
Leaving of it only vocal trace ;
As it prayeth soars above the mind,
Lifting to the Heavens a new-born face.

BY THE LIMES.

THE welkin burned with glowing ray
What time hot June sped on her way
In flaming chariot of the Sun,
Drawn by the Hours untiring on,
When I went forth to greet the day,
And watch these Hours at sportive play.

With laugh and song the welkin rung,
And balmy airs around they flung;
The fleecy cloud before them flew,
And soon was driven from my view;
While, as they drove in rapid gyre,
Their censers pour'd the flowing fire.

So went I forth the Nymph to see
Thus riding in high ecstasy;
And, being less ethereal found,
I sought where shaded was the ground,
When met my thought some pleasant limes,
Where sounding were delicious chimes.

So by the limes I took my way,
All soul to hear that charming lay;
And now within the vernal cope
The fount of sound did on me ope;
For, raised afore my dancing eye,
I saw the bower of lullaby.

Above, around, with matchless grace,
A wingèd choir fill'd all the place;
Now drinking nectar from the flower,
With sweetest fragrance brimming o'er;
Now pouring forth a murmurous sound,
Till changed the spot to Fairy ground.

And as the common light did fade
Before the sheen that choir had made,
My soul, transfigured by the sight,
And smitten with the music's might,
Did melt, and sigh herself away,
And radiant woke in endless day.

A SUNSET PICTURE.

From my window, open thrown,
Looking toward the setting sun,
Musing with my books alone,
When my daily task was done :

Gaily met my wandering gaze,
Where it never show'd before,
In the dreamy twilight haze,
Placid lake and mountain shore.

Glassy was its loving breast,
Gently flowing in the light,
Soothing too its dulcet rest,
Rippling softly to the night.

Fail'd it only swelling sail,
Bearing proudly toward the strand,
Telling sweetly lover's tale
Speeding swiftly to the land.

Still, though flowing there alone,
Gliding none upon its breast,
Was not all its beauty thrown
On a desert unconfess'd.

Saw the rosy light its grace,
Giving first the beauteous form,
Saw my soul its glorious face,
Blushing deep with colours warm.

Placid lake, in Beauty's form,
Making musical the night,
Livest thou where blows no storm,
Image of th' Eternal Light.

A VISION OF CHILDHOOD.

THE calm and clear repose of summer night
The weary world did soothe with balmy sleep;
The Pleiads shed sweet influence on the deep,
When shone upon my soul a marvellous light.

Some light, whose essence was not sun or star,
Whereby weak Nature speaks with stammering tongue
And cheats the stumbling sense the dead among,
And stirs in man deep internecine war;

But light that sought me from the far beyond—
A wayward child, then tranced in realms unseen—
And showed my wondering eye a dazzling sheen
Where rising choirs of angels sat enthroned.

A light that inly searched my spirit through,
And pierced my thought at will, as wholly known,
And bore me on, and left me all alone,
And o'er my brow drew forth a streaming dew.

Some light which rapt me to a distant day,
And brought my soul to stand at Judgment's bar,
And seemed to place me from the Judge afar
As one who cumber'd much that awful way.

Yet beam'd in all that pure and lustrous light
A tender joy from all those loving eyes,
And straight mine heart did melt in sobs and sighs,
And now I ceased to tremble at the sight.

My soul no longer fail'd me in the night,
For in those eyes sweet Mercy spake, and said,
" Eternal Love hath call'd thee from the dead,
So follow thou the Lamb in vestment white."

AN EVENING MEDITATION.

THE sun was sinking low in Whitehorse Vale,
What time the grain was golden in the field,
The milkmaid cross'd my sight with flowing pail
As strove mine eye to pierce that burning shield.

Quick thoughts newborn in Childhood's dreamy hour
In rapid stream flow'd out upon my soul,
And on her thrilling sense their forms did pour,
While deep within a magic feeling stole.

And shall that fading light, I said, so fair,
Which late did fill and guide this circling sphere,
This soul confine within this narrow air,
And think for aye to keep me captive here?

Shall dim-eyed Twilight of the shadowy eve,
With noiseless footstep gliding from the West,
For ever bind her in the night to grieve,
And shall my striving spirit ne'er find rest?

Beyond that failing orb now sinking low
And seeking sleep upon the placid wave,
Oh, shines there not a light of purer glow
Where evermore the darkness finds its grave;

Beyond that waning light in realms unseen,
Above the mystic stair that Jacob clomb,
Oh, spreads there not for aye the dazzling sheen
Where calmly dwells the soul as in her Home.

SABBATH BELLS.

HARK, my soul, the Sabbath bells are chiming,
Through the lattice sweet their voices flow,
Seems it much this room is too confining,
I to church this morn will thoughtful go.

Deep my soul within I hear them ringing,
Sinks their solemn music in my breast,
Seems it of some higher world they're singing
Where the spirit dwells in placid rest.

Rapt their mystic strains awake a longing
High to soar beyond the reach of Time,
And, with spirits stellar spaces thronging,
Taste in full the sweetness of their chime.

Hush'd in soft repose the air is listening,
Breathing lowly as a child in sleep,
Gentlier flows the light with temper'd glistening,
As the sounds ascend the azure deep.

Seems it as I walk this holy morning
Whither calls my soul this solemn chant,
Weeping Nature is herself adorning
While stayeth she her cry of deep lament.

Hark, my soul, the chimes are fast expiring,
In God's temple only canst thou rest,
There, His saints among in worship blending,
Joy shall find thee gilding all thy west.

WITH NIGHT ALONE.

ALONE, alone with dark and solemn night,
Deep hush'd the Sense to Nature's ebb and flow.
All outer sight and sound indrawn with light,
And gentle Zephyr only whispering low.

Alone, alone, in silence of the soul,
When stealthy comes the mystic spell of sleep ;
And 'fore the eyes a dreamy mist doth roll,
And spirits weird do haunt the airy deep.

Alone, alone, deep musing all alone,
My stirring thought awake, and bent to know,
All bonds I broke, and walk'd the inner zone,
Where grief and care no gloomy shadows throw.

Alone, alone, I trod the realm of mind,
Far stretching, where no sun or star is seen,
Where reaches not Earth's chill and wailing wind.
Nor mingles e'er its darkness with the sheen.

Alone, alone, in this deep realm alone,
Which seemèd to my soul an awful place,
I sought where flamed afar the burning throne,—
I sought where shone Eternal Beauty's face.

Alone, alone, I wended high my flight,
And pass'd the bounds where Space and Time do meet,
I soarèd upward ever to the light,
Yet all too weak that glorious Face to greet.

Alone, alone, I sped the dreadful way,
While ever as I rose that Face did rise,
Far, far beyond the fount of finite day,
High, high above the arc of astral skies.

Alone, alone, by mighty love upborne,
Yet tremulous and weak with fear untold,
I strove to reach the confines of the bourne
Where shone the light of ruby and of gold.

Alone, alone, I kept the dazzling line,
Though fail'd my sight, ill-temper'd to the ray,
For longed I much to see that Face divine,
Transfiguring with light my mortal clay.

Alone, alone, I bore me high and far,
Strong Faith upholding, as the soul did fall;
Till rose that light beyond, a glorious Star,
And drew me on with life-inspiring call.

Alone at last, no longer with the night,
My soul, as weary child on mother's breast,
Her wings did fold upon that gentle light,
And slept as doth the bird in downy nest.

Alone at last no longer in the deep,
For kingly Christ that Star did fill the place;
I saw, and loved Him in that balmy sleep,
I woke, and on me shone His Holy Face.

A MORNING WALK.

On a dewy morning early,
When the autumn sun was waking,
And was all my lattice pearly,
Went I forth, my couch forsaking.

Bracing was the air and cheery,
Fragrant odours crept around me;
Heard I, saw I, nothing weary
Moving in my company.

Sparkled russet leaf and flower,
With a dewy light refreshing;
Drank the thirsty woods the dower,
Fallen on them with caressing.

Lay my path across the barley,
Gay and golden in the morning,
Glad to greet me walking early,
Bending gently to my roaming.

Walking thus, and lightly musing,
Woke mine ear a music thrilling,
Sweetly soul and sense confusing,
From a tiny warbler welling.

Upward strove the song ascending,
Deepening fondly in its rising,
To the choral angels wending,
Weird and wondrous, all surprising.

Seem'd it to my soul entrancèd,
Rapt away in mystic dreaming,
That the sweetness grew enhancèd
By some radiant Presence gleaming :

Seem'd it that some lyric angel
Passing by, on mission holy,
Gave the song its high Evangel,
Blending with its music wholly :

Seem'd it that the bird perceiving
Flamy wings above it hovering,
Soar'd beyond the soul's conceiving,
Where appears no fleshly covering :

Seem'd it that at music's fountain,
Drinking sound from seraphs flowing,
Clung it to the heavenly mountain,
Lower joys of earth foregoing :

Seem'd it that my soul was moving
In a realm where springs the morning,
Borne there by that songster loving,
In a moment reft of warning :

Seem'd it to my ardent longing,
As the glorious bird kept singing,
Fled was all of Earth's belonging
All its Babel ceaseless ringing :

Seem'd it that my soul, forgetting
All it knew of darksome feeling,
Ne'er should see the sun's downsetting
With dim twilight on her stealing.

MY HOME BY THE POPLARS.

STATELY Poplar, looking from the hill,
Greeting kindly in the breezy morn,
Gladly do I court thy friendly will
Ever with the circling day re-born.

Stately Poplar, shining in the light,
Waving o'er thy silvery arms in joy,
Warmly do I blend in thy delight,
Keenly suffer what may thee annoy.

Stately Poplar, bending to the breeze,
Whispering softly in an undertone,
Gently die thy murmurs on the leas,
Pouring on the air sweet orison.   .

Stately Poplar, looking up to Heaven,
Inly breathing forth thy mystic prayer,
Seems it deeply thou'rt a symbol given,
Wafting music on the trancèd air.

Stately Poplar, wedded to my soul,
Blending wholly with its gentle flow,
Ever to me thy low whispers roll,
Even as to thee they come and go.

Stately Poplar, form of beauty known.
Proudly reaching up the azure dome,
Graceful art thou in thy speech and tone,
Much I love thee smiling on my home.

PAGANINI BY THE SEA.

WHERE rise Genoa's palaces of stone,
Their stately forms projecting on the sea,
E'en there, where song and music long have shone,
And soothed the trancèd air with melody,—

Upon a still and dreamy Summer eve,
That pour'd a golden glory on the wave,
What time dim twilight makes the breast to heave
With love that springs immortal from the grave,—

Two children sported on the sounding shore,
And yearning drank with quick and subtle ear
What sung the tide, discoursing evermore
Of things whose essence is the upper sphere.

Their souls drawn forth by witchery of tone,
Whereby the spirit shows its hidden life,
They mused and communed with the sea alone,
They pondered long upon its solemn strife.

They saw the sun go down in mellow light,
They saw the silvery moon awake the dome,
Yet still they clung with fondness to the night,
Nor cared to hie them to their gentle home.

The boy, a slender form of pallid mien,
With searching eye that flashed a fiery ray,
And soul that in the face did radiant gleam,
And give the music of a sunny day;

The girl, a beauteous flower of fragrant breath,
Where rose and lily strove their grace to blend,
And amaranth did seem to mock at death,
With nought its merry laugh and song to rend.

There stood they by the sea, all rapt and lone,
Intent the secret of its voice to know,
Till stirred within the thought of other tone,
And Art withdrew them from its murmurs low.

So Nature in her outer flow did pass,
Yet only to return within their soul,
On whose fair disc as in an optic glass
Her severed forms were blent in perfect whole.

Thus winsome Nature brought they with them home,
And with her sights and sounds they nurtured grew;
Yet still above her mountain heights they clomb,
And strength and joy transcending hers they drew.

The ardent boy it was who most did cling
The lofty music of the wave to wed,
And oft at night he'd wake to hear it sing
And drink the mystic voices which it shed.

For in high Music's realm he had his birth,
And nourish'd was with every dulcet sound;
He caught each sweetness as it roam'd the Earth,
And drew consenting harmonies from the ground.

So now at light of Moon by Art call'd home,
He stood with lattice open to the sea,
And she who oft and far with him did roam
Did with him drink again its melody.

And as the sounding shore its anthem sung,
And sent its murmurs to their listening ear,
The boy his viol took down from where it hung,
While trembled in his eye deep Passion's tear.

As living thing he kiss'd its thrilling form,
And strain'd it to his breast in burning love;
Then swept its chords, replying to the storm,
And subtly passing to the cooing dove.

With magic hand he touch'd the trembling strings,
With flaming soul he woke its witching tone;
Till seized the growing sound strong eagle's wings,
And bore them far beyond Earth's narrow zone.

And now descending from the heights of Song,
And pausing in an interval of sound,
There ran a Spider from the vines among,
That with fond tendrils round the lattice wound.

With fine æsthetic sense the spirit came
To view that wondrous Artist playing there;
For she, too, kindled to the music's flame,
While heaved her bosom to the mighty prayer.

Yet look'd the stranger at the blue-eyed girl,
As if her laughing Presence barr'd the way,
As if she stay'd high Passion's eddying whirl,
By lightly pouring in the glare of day.

So sat she far apart in dainty spleen,
And waited till the child the room did quit,
And burst again the music from its screen,
When near the pulsing strings she fearless lit.

"Good evening, beauteous Silvercup," he cried,
And set her joyous on the quivering frame;
Then sought again where deep his Muse did hide,
And led her forth all girt with brilliant flame.

Once more the magic sounds their hiding left,
From out the dome of Night inspired they came;
The airy sea with noiseless wing they cleft,
And sung anew rapt Music's glorious name.

PAGANINI BY THE SEA.

Far in the night the Artist woo'd his lyre,
Till thrill'd the very walls with Passion's joy ;
While drank that tiny form the pulsing fire,
As one who tastes a bliss which ne'er can cloy.

So sped the hours till rose the Star of day,
The lovers join'd by mystic ties of sound,
When each at last did take a sever'd way,
And trod they once again the common ground.

Thus in the "golden prime," by that blue Sea,
And from the lattice looking on its wave,
These three did wed with lofty minstrelsy,
And each to each love's holy blessing gave.

But now for azure sky and whispering air,
There came a clouded dome with wailing sigh,
And burning fever smote the damsel fair,
And rent their budding life with tragic cry.

Yet ere she passed that clouded dome beyond,
And in the shining Morning Land did wake,
She sought the Artist who, with touches fond,
Such weird and wondrous harmony could make.

With viol in hand he stood beside her bed,
With rapid glance divined the maiden's call ;
And woke a strain to love celestial wed,
So sweet that broke it nigh Death's icy thrall.

What have I said I stint that Artist's might,
For Death, as arm'd with sharp and potent sting,
Shrunk back before the pure and rhythmic light,
Nor moved while soar'd the boy on flaming wing.

But Life, warm gushing from the inner deep,
Found trumpet voice, and said in lofty tone,
"Sweet darling, I this eve shall yield to sleep,
And for a fleeting hour leave thee alone.

" I hear the Angels call my soul away,
And shall I pass within Time's blinding veil;
But thou shalt rise a radiant Star of day,
And in high Music's realm shall proudly sail."

In calm prophetic tone her thought she told,
And sought athwart the arc the bowers of rest :
While he, as sheep that's sunder'd from the fold,
Now roam'd the World alone in clouded west.

Yet one friend loving soothed his stricken soul,
And gently calm'd the swelling of the stream ;
For e'er as o'er that disc dim sadness stole,
And shone the higher light with feeble gleam,

And sought the Artist in his withering grief,
To chase the gloom with Music's balmy light,—
Then stood that Spider forth in fond relief,
And shared the striving hours till fled the night.

Thus lived the twain—the Spider and the boy,
Thus rose in solemn hours unearthly strains ;
Thus thrill'd their sense as one to gushing joy,
And roam'd weird voices far across the plains.

E'en thus high festival they constant kept,
Till burst the quivering strings all finite bound :
When on the lyre for aye the Spider slept,
And Paganini wept, yet bless'd the sound.

THE MYSTERY OF SOUND.

AT early morn, when glowing June is near,
With florid beauty in her dancing eye,
Awoke a mystic sound mine inner ear,
And drew my breast to heave with gentle sigh.

My thrilling sense it struck with stifled groan,
As though its essence dwelt within my soul ;
I mused, and inly sought at Reason's throne
Why this strange sound had subtly o'er me stole.

Again, and still again, low toned it spoke,
But not as yet with clear articulate tone ;
All ear, I caught the slow recurring stroke,
I strove, but could not reach its inner zone.

E'er as it came along the murmurous wind,
I sought to read the word it stealthy brought,
I searched in vain the mighty realm of mind—
In vain I wrestled with my baffled thought :

Perplex'd, but not as yet bereft of hope,
I dived to depths which underlie the Thought;
I trod a brighter sphere, and radiant woke,
And found the hidden answer that I sought.

In this deep Realm, where awful Love is known,
And in dread silence rise the springs of Life,
I saw in concrete form that stifled moan,
A bleeding Nymph, struck down with treacherous knife:

A bleeding Nymph, of sad and pallid mien,
Whose dwelling was the green and flowing mead;
With modest cowslips there she walked unseen,
And from their nectar'd sweets her soul did feed.

To blinded Sense a sacrifice she fell,
As late with cold relentless scythe in hand
The heedless mower swept the wavy dell,
And pour'd her life-blood on the vernal strand.

Thus stricken down in all her maiden grace,
That moan I learnt was her expiring cry;
And still with mournful sound it filled the place,
Ascending ever to the listening sky.

That mournful sound, I deeply hear it still,
And seems it much to mean the plaint of Life;
It strikes upon the centre of my will,
And binds my bleeding soul to that dread knife.

THE POET'S EYE.

THERE are who feign the Poet's eye in frenzy rolls.
As if high Passion flow'd a dark and turbid stream :
But is the Poet's eye the subtle eye of souls,
Who see in clearest day the glorious things they dream ?

When yet did whirling Frenzy mingle in the light
By which from airy crag the Eagle views the sun ?
When did that piercing flame take on the mist of night.
And feebly gleam as dying lamp whose course is run ?

When yet did darksome Frenzy rend the lofty brow
Where majesty reposes in the lion's face ?
When was the forest-king e'er seen his head to bow.
As if reposeful strength had fled his noble race ?

Ah ! no, the Poet's eye doth burn with steadfast ray.
Congenerous for aye with intellective life ;
E'er moves it as the march of laughing blue-eyed Day,
With bounding joy and love and radiant beauty rife.

The Poet's eye doth rise where dawns the dewy East,
And flows all day with song, high Music's joy confess'd :
With reason sharp and clear, and mighty love doth feast,
And sets at dreamy eve in glories of the West.

Far swiftlier than the light e'er moves the Poet's eye,
And sheds sweet radiance down upon the wondering Race :
With free and boundless sweep it soars from sky to sky,
And shines it as before from rapturous Prophet's face.

With searching glance it looks deep in the heart of things,
And reaches unto that which lies within the veil ;
With conscious strength it weighs the boastful acts of kings,
And shows how Truth and Love alone at last prevail.

The Poet's eye enthroned as lofty Seer of God,
From heavenly hills notes all below the sun ;
And with high scorn and hate, e'en as with fiery rod,
It scathes all grovelling souls who in base courses run.

The Poet's eye, oh, it is flame and light in one,
And flows it deep and strong afar in crystal seas ;
And highest Music makes its rolling unison,
And floods alike dim wallèd towns and breezy leas.

The Poet's eye, rare essence strong, and quick and pure,
High servant is for evermore to Truth and Right ;
Athwart the wrecks of Time it reigns for ever sure,
E'er rising calm and clear 'mid all the stormy night.

AN AUTUMN LAY.

SWEET Autumn's come, dear Autumn's here,
In cloud and field her form I see ;
She reigns in all this northern sphere,
She's on the land, she's on the sea.

Oh, stately is the Autumn queen,
With slow and silent step she moves ;
And oft puts on a golden sheen,
As run her wheels in golden grooves.

I see her colour'd light around,
Upon the wood, upon the lea ;
With flowing robe she sweeps the ground,
While singeth low her minstrelsy.

With intermittent note they sing
Who ere she came filled all the grove :
For dream the birds on tranced wing,
And pour the strain from riper love.

Oh, beauteous is the Autumn maid,
In all the Faëry realm around ;
Pours she rich purple on the glade,
All blent with gurgling waters' sound.

Sweet is the maid, I've known her long,
A virgin she from worlds afar,
Down-coming with high Seraph's song,
And glory of the Evening Star.

Dear is the maid, I love her well,
I've woo'd her now for many a year ;
And many griefs she'th heard me tell,
And with her hair wiped many a tear.

Soft is the maid, I know her touch,
I've felt her arms about my neck ;
Dear, tender soul, I love her much,
Nor have I seen or flaw or fleck.

Serene with heavenly joy she's dight,
And sweetly tells of realms unseen ;
She draws me to the upper light,
And fills me with her golden sheen.

Dear Autumn maid, I've loved thee long.
I'll love thee more another day ;
Till I am free take this my song,
And keep it as an Autumn lay.

A MOONLIT SEA.

THE full-orb'd Moon shone high above the deep,
What time the Summer night was calm and clear ;
Nor came anigh the drowsy car of sleep,
For woke the murmurous Sea my tranced ear.

Where rises Sandown cliff above the strand,
And showeth fair and sweet with stretching bay,
In Wight's dear Isle so like the Faëry land,
Whose skies are ever blue with laughing day,—

There sat I looking out upon the night,
From crystal doors thrown open wide I saw ;
And drank my thirsty soul the dreamy light,
And mused I long and deep on Beauty's law.

In ample dome of soft and shadowy blue,
The silvery Moon majestic held the throne ;
And in my soul more fair and queenly grew,
As swept she on in radiant Beauty's zone.

There walked she in the stilly night alone,
All sound and sight of busy day afar;
There joyous heard that Sea's low murmurous tone.
This goddess high—of night the peerless star.

Uprose the mystic music of the deep,
As wave on wave did gently strike the shore;
And with the strain my soul went up the steep,
And to high Heaven I came as through a door.

To Heaven, I say, my soul ascended straight,
Borne up on airy wings of murmurous sound;
For there in all the Worlds is that high gate,
Where soars the rapturous soul above the ground.

So there to Beauty's realm in awe I came,
And shone that Moon with high transfigured face;
Seem'd it her light now blent with golden flame,
As more and more she fill'd with Beauty's grace.

And now as in the silence of the night
The plaintive music of the sea uprose,
Nor could dissever'd be from this sweet light,
But blended were as fragrance and the rose.

My soul already rapt in dreamy spheres,
Took on a higher form of complex life;
For awful Beauty fill'd both eyes and ears,
And Passion felt and own'd the double strife.

Sweet strife of Sense with joy for common root,
Fair mystic Moon, low murmurous mystic sea;
Upon an Eden night I pluck'd ambrosial fruit,
Alone with dreamy light and minstrelsy.

Alone in that ideal sphere I dream'd,
While Beauty held my soul in silent awe;
No longer denizen of earth I seem'd,
Nor could I find to utter what I saw.

There swept the queenly Moon along the night,
There woo'd the Sea her beams with Music's sound,
There swam my soul upon the flowing light,
Till showed again the colour of the ground.

MY POPLARS.

COME, see my Poplars on the hill,
All ye who Beauty know and feel;
Come, see them with soft breezes fill,
And seeing, let your sorrows heal.

In Autumn's mellow light they shine
With blended lines of gold and green;
Oh, man, I would my bliss were thine
As now I view that mystic sheen.

With rustlings as of Angels' wings
Their branches tremble in the light,
I look and fly all earthly things,
I soar where cometh not the night.

On dreamy wings I soar away,
Transfigured by that lucid wave;
I drink the springs of laughing day,
And dewy joy my soul doth lave.

Oh, beauteous is that flowing light
That gently stirs these Poplar leaves;
It melts my soul, it fills my sight,
It showeth fair as golden sheaves.

And with the light sweet music flows,
As of the wave upon the shore,
When soft and low it murmurous goes,
Of love discoursing evermore.

And with the sound entranced I pass
Where sings that Sea the lover's song,
And see as in an optic glass,
And hear its wooing all day long.

Oh, glorious is the play of light,
Oh, wondrous is the thrill of sound;
Fly on, dear soul, and quit the night,
No more return to common ground.

Come, see my Poplars on the hill,
All ye who weary are of Town;
Come drink the light and feel the thrill,
And no more grieve, and no more frown.

Come, see the place where Freedom dwells;
Come, see the spot where Peace retires;
Come, walk abroad in leafy dells,
And light anew low burning fires.

TO MADELINE.

To thee, who eighteen summers gone
From upper skies didst gently glide,
And on thy mother sweetly shone,
And Joy's high gates didst open wide,—

To thee who cam'st that Sabbath morn,
Bright vision of unclouded light,
And from our life didst pluck the thorn,
And chase before thee plaintive night,—

To thee who gav'st that happy day
A pledge of Eden-bliss return'd,
And charm'd us with thy sunny ray,
While with ecstatic praise we burn'd,—

Madeline, to thee my Song ascends,
It climbs the heights where thou dost shine.
To catch as up the are it wends
Some sweetness from thy face benign.

To thee, thou child of heavenly birth,
A queenly woman grown to-day,
With eye compact of thoughtful mirth,
And soul that soars in lofty way.

To thee, thou noble, loving child,
On whose calm brow pale beauty gleams,
And waits in gentle mood and mild
To stir thy fancy with her dreams.

And high-soul'd thought there finds a throne,
And grandly reigns from morn to eve,
And loveth much that sweep of zone,
Ascending air without reprieve.

Where dwelleth more celestial love,
Thy face suffusing with its tide,
Down-flowing from the sea above,
From Earth beneath divided wide.

Madeline, to thee my Song doth fly,
With mystic rose and lily dight,
And greets thee in thine azure sky,
And sighs to mingle in the light.

To thee it soars, to thee it clings,
Inflamèd with thy subtle fire;
With thee it wends on golden wings,
To thee it strikes the joyous lyre.

WEBER'S LAST WALTZ.

" Give me the lyre," von Weber, dying, said,
" And let my fingers sweep its golden strings ;
Let Music's rapture fill mine heart and head,
Ere angels bear me far on rushing wings.

" Let heavenly airs from high seraphic spheres
Flow down in dulcet waves upon my soul,
And joy outflow in Passion's burning tears,
And rend from Time and Space their dark control.

" Let mystic dreams of sweet euphonious sound,
Mine ears anoint with numbers soft and low,
And let my spirit inly there be found
Where on the crystal sea rapt harpers glow.

" Where on the glassy sea with harps of gold
They pour immortal strains of gushing love,
And hymn His praises who from days of old
Hath been as He is still—life's quickening Dove.

"There will I seize all sweet and rhythmic strains,
And trace their law back to its hidden springs,
And draw them downward to these lower plains,
And mix them with the World's inferior things.

" With lower things of earth I'll join the airs
Ere from my hands doth fail the joyous lyre;
With mortal sighs I'll mix undying prayers,
To man's cold love I'll add the living fire."

Thus, dying, Weber said, and struck the chords;
With fiery hand he swept the quivering strings,
And listening Music heard his glowing words,
And even held the lyre as one who sings.

Her hand his hand within the lyre she held
(For flow'd she on his soul at every pore),
And 'woke its life as Orpheus did of eld,
And to her inner realm did ope the door.

Where heavenliest harmonies do dwell she ope'd,
And flow'd their sweetness in upon his soul,
And Passion with ethereal Fancy yoked,
And blent—their essence made one perfect whole.

So wave on wave of glorious music flow'd,
And Weber drank athirst the burning tide,
And evermore with deeper passion glow'd,
As Fancy ope'd her beauteous temple wide.

Struck he the golden strings as one inspired,
And strove with high desire his heart to sing,
And more and more was all within him fired
As Fancy bore him up on flaming wing.

Sung he of Love, great goddess of the World,
Of Love supremely good, divinely fair,
As saw he high her banners bright unfurl'd,
And sweetly thrilling all the upper air.

Of Love he sung in highest beauty dight,
In flowing robes of gold and sapphire sheen,
Of mighty Love, diaphanous with light,
Of human souls the dear celestial Queen.

Her beauteous eyes of deepest azure blue
Shone softly on him from her radiant throne,
And up the dazzling heights the music flew,
And winged soar'd at will from zone to zone.

Felt he their tender shining on his soul,
And all his being melted 'neath the ray ;
Strove he anew to rise and touch the goal,
Where gently break the springs of endless day.

Saw he her lips the spell of silence loose,
While listen'd all the air with breath indrawn ;
Heard he the dulcet tones of Heaven's high Muse,
Downflowing from the chambers of the morn.

Again he struck the chords with Passion's hand,
And deeper in his soul the music ran;
Yearn'd he to wake in rosy Morning Land,
Where new-born souls soft breezes lightly fan.

Thus, dying Weber sang his parting lay,
While hovering yet within the bounds of Time,
And left a strain that deathless is for aye,
And shall be sweeter heard in fairer clime.

To rhythmic step he wrought the glorious strain,
To grace of gliding feet he set the bars,
And left a music fit for Love's refrain,
That echoes evermore among the Stars.

High Music, soft and sweet, and calm and pure,
Great prophecy of love without alloy,
Athwart the wrecks of Time shalt thou endure,
And radiant Weber crown with rapturous joy.

MOZART'S REQUIEM.

Rest thou, oh weary soul, rapt Mozart sung,
Sleep thou as infant on the mother's breast ;
Let dark regrets afar from thee be flung,
The golden hour has come, the hour of rest.

Rest thou, dear soul, from whelming storms of Time,
Whose crested billows long have broke thy sleep ;
Let's haste away and seek the sunny clime,
Where Peace doth rule for aye the upper deep.

With lyre in hand 'gin we to take the flight,
Where Music's presence sweet doth fill the sphere ;
Where interfused she moves in all the light,
And rapturous songs doth sing from year to year.

With lyre in hand we'll climb the lofty stair
That slopeth upward through the dark of night ;
With joyous strains we'll seek the morning air,
And Music shall upbear us in the flight.

Take rest, dear soul, the rest of lyric love,
Deep flowing as the lake of base unfound;
For Music's joy as peace is known above,
And all the rapture there is Music's sound.

In peace repose, the stilly peace of God,
For Earth no more our stricken heart shall rend;
Lean thou, my soul, upon His mighty rod,
And boldly fly where doth the spiral wend.

Where the far spiral climbs from deep to deep,
Through lyric choirs ascending evermore,
There let us rise and quit this mortal sleep,
And sing the lofty songs of that blest shore.

And with each wingèd word he struck the lyre,
With mighty hand he struck the quivering strings;
And knew they well that subtle touch of fire,
And strove to sing in turn celestial things.

And things celestial sounded from the chords,
And still do echo through the realms of space;
For inmost Passion spake in burning words,
As strove the lyre to soothe the tragic Race.

Of that fair stream the rapturous Music sung,
That floweth out upon th' Eternal Throne;
Where round about the beauteous rainbow's hung,
Sweet type, how loving is the Holy One!

Of that dear stream there flowing soft and clear,
That maketh glad for aye the saints of God;
And beauty giveth all in that bright sphere,
While decks its banks the budding almond rod.

Of this great Mozart sung, with soul aflame,
As to his inner eye it shone above,
And strove the pulsing lyre to sound its name,
And show how all the stream is quickening love.

Dear glorious love, unquenchable for aye,
High flowing there with calm and peaceful wave;
And making heavenliest music all the day,
And giving might to all who in it lave.

" By that still water, oh my weary soul,
Thou'lt taste anon the sweets of endless rest;
For going art thou far from Earth's control,
And soon thy wings shalt fold in downy nest.

"To that calm water let us haste away,
And drink deep draughts of peace for evermore;
For here dim night e'er drowns the struggling day,
And rending Discord cleaves to every shore.

"To that still water, flowing soft and deep,
God's angels soon shall bear us through the air;
Let then high Music wake us out of sleep,
And all our thought and life be lyric prayer.

"With Music's joy we'll climb the airy steeps,
To thrilling sound of lyre the journey make:
In Music's flow'ring robe ascend the deeps,
And as we soar the stellar spaces wake.

" Rest thee, dear soul, I sing to thee of rest,
From broken lights and jarring sounds we go:
I see the glory failing in the West,
Up to the kindling East we soon shall flow,

" Where shineth fair and calm beyond the sun.
The glorious light which no beginning knows:
And rest remains for all whose race is run,
Where deep and calm that stilly water flows.

" There, oh my soul, we're sweetly called away,
Low voices tell it to mine inner ear;
Arise, dear soul, for breaks Eternal Day,
Why should we walk alone in sorrow here?"

BEETHOVEN'S GRAND MARCH.

WHEN yearning manhood strove within my soul,
What time its budding leaf began to ope,
And burning Passion sought high Freedom's goal,
And War and Love all glorious in me woke;

And all my thought, as flew each golden hour,
The lonely bounds of night essay'd to break,
And soar where is for aye the realm of power,
And lyric choirs one heavenly music make.

When full and free the mystic tide of life
A river swift and strong did deeply flow,
And new-born sweetness found with joy of wife,
As confluent stream of love discoursing low.

In that sweet time of Spring, long, long ago,
When not as yet the World had broke my sleep,
Nor woke my scorn with idle pomp and show,
For that I had not then look'd on the deep.

The cold and gloomy deep, wherein it lies,
To treacherous Hate close wed for evermore :
Ne'er looking upward to the joyous skies,
Nor dreaming of the Sea without a shore.

In that fond time, when now the westering sun
In golden splendours sought the placid wave,
And joy'd to know the glorious race he'd run,
And 'gan afresh to rise as from the grave.

There sounded in mine ear a wondrous strain,
All sweetly blended with the failing light ;
Seem'd it to open on a boundless plain,
And distant journey take athwart the night.

From stately harp of high and solemn sound
The music pour'd in quick successive stream,
And bore me far beyond earth's narrow ground,
And fill'd my soul with Battle's lofty dream.

Struck were the golden chords with lily hands,
That rhythmic motion took with easy grace ;
Showed they she dwelt in Music's tuneful lands,
Who thus the strings did sweep in rapid race.

From lily hands the glorious music came,
From Passion's heaving breast I saw it flow ;
What wonder that my soul uprose in flame,
And with that lofty music sought to go ?

O'er mountains dark and cold it led the way,
Athwart wide burning sands the march went on ;
Seem'd it to strive where stilly breaks the day
That follows on the night when victory's won.

Across the sounding sea it wingèd flew,
And rose its thrilling note beyond its roar ;
With every pulsing string the music grew,
And seem'd it far to seek some distant shore.

From gilded halls, where Luxury reclines,
And pamper'd frets from weary morn to eve ;
From Mammon's dismal cells where light ne'er shines,
And Penury doth silken garments weave ;

From cold exclusive cloisters' freezing shade,
Where Genius rapt is slain in act of birth ;
And men with dusty learning mad are made,
And mocking Death too oft doth strangle worth ;

From grovelling haunts of Science, falsely named,
Where sciolists do prate in unknown tongue,
And idol thrones with hideous noise are claim'd,
And shallow brains with futile toil are wrung ;

From pits of Hell, where base-born greed is found,
And with its wares doth mix the unctuous lie,
And poison sows in all the groaning ground,
Nor dreams the lie is known from sky to sky;

From all this false and fever'd whirl of life,
That makes that wretched thing we call the World,
Beethoven bids us march with flashing knife,
While to the breeze the flag of War's unfurl'd.

Loud echoes evermore its martial strain,
And calls us up to Battle's lofty field,
E'er up the air ascends its grand refrain :
"Smite thou the wrong —the right uphold and shield."

Prepare, Oh, World ! that mighty strain to hear,
For will the glorious trumpet soon awake ;
For Christ doth lead apace the golden year,
And soon in ire shall thrones and sceptres shake.

Full soon, Oh, World ! He'll break thy treacherous sleep,
And tread the wine-press of His righteous hate ;
Rise up, Oh, World ! and march thou through the deep,
And strive by death to win ere yet too late.

TO IONÈ.

Ionè of the laughing eye,
Ionè of the archèd brow ;
They tell me that thy birthday's nigh,
Though I believe it's gone just now.

The first is gone, the tenth is here,
And soon to woman thou'lt be grown ;
And I would now awake thine ear
With flowing Music's lyric tone.

But first observe her glorious form,
Within thy soul in beauty clad ;
For soon she'll take the wings of storm,
Though gentle now, and calm and glad.

For Music is a lofty dame,
With soul the lead hath never found ;
And moves she in the fiery flame,
And dwells alone in pulsing sound.

And much as thou her mood doth change,
As fly the Hours in rapid gyre ;
Now sounding notes all weird and strange,
Now breathing low her subtle fire.

A glorious maid of queenly grace,
She rules an empire broad and deep ;
The radiant Sun dwells in her face,
The dreamy Moon attends her sleep.

With feet too dainty for the ground
And soul that scorns this narrow air,
She walks the welkin round and round,
And dwells where soars our highest prayer.

So, Music, seek my little maid,
And be for aye her lofty child,
And so thou ne'er shalt walk in shade
Nor fear in days when clouds are wild.

High Music wed thee to thy soul,
And drink her life as flowers the dew ;
So shalt thou touch the shining goal
Where thou shalt e'er thy youth renew ;

The shining goal in Heaven afar
High floating o'er the crystal sea,
Rising beyond the highest star,
A column vast of melody.

AYLMER'S FIELD.

Of Aylmer's Field the lofty Poet sung,
And gave a strain that deathless is for aye ;
And Music sweetly round about him hung,
And Joy and Love did pour the glorious lay.

With fiery hand he struck the glowing lyre,
And swept high scorn and hate the pulsing chords,
And nobly told the Prophet's awful ire,
And utter'd swift his thought in burning words.

Of Aylmer's Field the soaring music sung,
That darksome place where Mammon holds his own,
And feeds on husks the grovelling swine among,
And bows him low at Satan's tinsel throne.

Of that foul place high warning hath he given,
And shown how that it is the field of blood ;
The tragic field, where human hearts are riven,
The field where grief and care do make the food.

The barren field wherein no flower will grow,
Nor e'er was seen fair Autumn's golden grain ;
But all the place is cold with arctic snow,
And Winter evermore doth gloom the plain.

Of Aylmer's Field he sung, and cursed the place,
With curse like that which fell from Israel's hill,
And shone high glory in his rapturous face
While kingly might upheld his striving will.

Of Aylmer's Field he sung with righteous hate
(Oh, wonder that poor man the place should love),
That knows no other God than chance or fate
And hath no blue and spreading heavens above.

Of Aylmer's Field he sung in words divine,
And sermon pour'd as Gothic temple old,
Ne'er drank afore, so sparkling is the wine,
So rich and clear the stream of flowing gold.

And Mammon from his curtain'd pew of pride,
For whom the text was found and sermon made,
For once did feel the life-blood softly glide,
For once did seek to hide him in the shade.

For knew he now what he had hid before,
How that all blind and bare he walked alone ;
As open'd to his eye the boundless shore
And rose the towering sky from zone to zone.

His pleasant pride, poor man, had merged in woe,
For she who should have kept his boasted name
No more his ear doth charm with murmurs low,
Or yield him as afore high dream of fame.

In all her virgin bloom and tender thought
She's pass'd from Mammon's narrow house afar,
She kept the faith—heroic fight she fought
And shineth evermore a beauteous star.

And he that long had sought her as his wife,
And won her love and loved her as his soul,
He too lies stricken there with murderous knife,
He too hath spurn'd low Mammon's darksome goal.

But startled Mammon now hath woke from sleep,
That mighty preacher there hath broke his rest ;
And Death had led afore from deep to deep,
And dim and lonesome was the failing west.

So now at last saw he with wakeful eye
What through the toiling years was hid before ;
How that his wretched life was all a lie,
A vain and idle show, and nothing more.

Of Aylmer's Field he sung, that Poet high,
And much I loved the bold and lofty strain ;
Ye winds, bear up his words from sky to sky,
And carry them afar o'er all the plain.

For Aylmer's Field I ween is vastly wide,
And many horrors doth it darkly keep;
But shall foul Mammon no more in it hide,
Or madly drown the soul in deadly sleep.

For hath the preacher said the place is waste,
And every house therein a house of woe;
Oh, Mammon, haste away, arise and haste,
E'en as the flying moments come and go.

RACHEL'S PRAYER.

"Oh, give me children or I die,"
Cried Rachel in dim Sorrow's hour ;
And up the azure strove the sigh,
And storm'd the Heavens with mighty power.

For children of the blood she pray'd,
A princely line to live for aye ;
For this she supplication made,
And saw the line in distant day.

In Vision's lofty field it shined,
A vast and glorious army grown,
(Its leader Christ, the King of mind.)
In serried ranks around the Throne.

And Rachel's prayer doth still arise,
And never more than now to-day,
When dark and gloomy are the skies,
And Hell doth block the Heavenly way.

From inward depths of striving souls
The orison doth wing its flight,
And all the day it upward rolls
And plaintive cries in dreams at night.

For children of the blood and brain
In this great dearth of truth and love,
For children born to live again
It ceaseless rends the Heavens above.

For high-soul'd thoughts and high-bred men
That mighty prayer doth e'er ascend ;
For blessing of the righteous ten
It doth untiring upward wend.

For queenly women, calm and fair,
With Summer and with Autumn crown'd.
E'er wafting music on the air
And shedding fragrance o'er the ground.

For children of immortal birth
Who sprung to life before the sun ;
And are but pilgrims on the earth,
Sojourners till their race is run.

For children sweet and guileless found,
Whose angels see the Father's face ;
Who think no thought nor utterance sound
That does not yearn to fold the Race.

For children striving to be just,
In all the complex web of life ;
Who use the gold as crumbling dust,
And smite the base with flashing knife.

For children meek and ever young,
With whom the Heavens do linger still ;
Who dwell the birds and flowers among,
In realms where is no cloud or chill.

For these the stricken World doth groan,
And Nature joineth in the cry ;
For these the Church doth pray alone,
" Oh, give me these, or else I die."

"FESTINA LENTÈ."

Oh, Man, high spirit, born to live for aye,
And tread the spaces of far worlds unseen ;
Immortal still though Time itself decay,
And inly bound about with golden sheen.

Rich heir to wealth beyond all mortal ken,
To things nor ear hath heard nor eye hath seen ;
Half angel now, a full-orb'd seraph then,
With soul endow'd high knowledges to glean.

Why fever'd is thy brow with mad desire ?
Why hasteth so thy soul in all the plain ?
Why runneth all thy blood with alien fire ?
Why cometh not reposeful calm again ?

Know'st not how in the Holy Book 'tis writ,
That every spirit strong who holds by faith,
Ne'er thinks or dreams by haste to grow in wit,
So firm his trust in what the Prophet saith.

And e'en the Pagan oracles of old,
By wise observance of the growing years,
Divined the truth with vision clear and bold,
That loss, not gain, doth flow from hurrying fears.

Then hasten slowly, ye who hasten will,
Eternal ages wait your work to see;
With single eye upclimb the heavenly hill,
And bear it with you there where live the free.

Yes, slowly hasten, thou, oh man of power,
Who king shalt thronèd be in realm of mind;
Nor fear the time when clouded is thine hour,
And thy high path thy fellows fail to find.

Art conscious in thyself thou'rt strong, dear soul?
That God hath made thee strong to speak His Name?
Then break thou every bond of earth's control,
And leave to meaner men the greed of fame.

The strong, dear soul, the strong do never haste,
But hold by faith that is both calm and sure;
Know they full well they're lonely in the waste,
Yet know they too their work shall long endure.

So hasten slowly, ye who strength desire,
If that you fain would bless the failing Race,
Let all your haste be that of holy fire,
And Christ shall put His glory on your face.

P

"ON THE WATERS."

Thy bread upon the waters cast,
  Thinker, toiling in the night ;
Thy guerdon thou shalt find at last,
  Sowing there Truth's golden light.

Dark hid within the mighty deep
  Long the precious grain may lie,
Yet shall it spring from out the sleep,
  Tending upward to the sky.

When many days have sped their flight,
  Circling upward to the sun,
A beauteous form of life and light
  Thee shall greet with orison.

From out the deep the grain shall spring,
  Leaving there its husky shell,
And glad the World a joyous thing,
  And of all thy labour tell.

So thou, strong thinker, by the deep,
   Toiling in the night alone,
Thy thought send forth, and no more weep.
   Hopeless of all benison.

Upon the waters cast the grain,
   Working in the mists of Time;
Behold it springs upon the main,
   Blooming in a fairer clime.

POET AND CRITIC.

Vex not thou the Poet's soul,
Critic, stumbling in the night,
For thou touchest not the goal
Whither tends that burning light.

Think thou not its force to mete,
Feebly crawling on the ground,
"For thou canst not fathom it,"
Nor its depths with plummet sound.

High it soars above the arc,
Deep it dives beneath the wave;
Be it thine in awe to hark,
Rising from thy narrow cave.

Bold and free it roams the sphere,
Asking none how it shall act,
Happy thou to note in fear
How it symbol finds in fact.

Pure and strong it wingèd flies
In the vast empyrean sea,
Flinging from it tears and sighs,
Ever rapt in ecstasy.

Critic, swimming on the stream,
Drifting onward to the main,
Wake thee from thy sluggish dream,
Reap by Faith earth's golden grain.

Mount thee with her to the Throne
Where the Angels lowly bend ;
Bow thee to the Holy One,
And with Seraphs' praises blend.

"WHAT IS THE WORLD?"

" WHAT is the World, papa?" he said,
A dark-eyed, laughing boy of seven;
" What is the World, and how's it fed;
Is it of earth, or come from Heaven?

" What is the World? I want to know—
You're always talking of the World;
Is it all bright with sunny glow,
And are blue banners there unfurl'd?

" Where is the World?" eke asked the child,
With hot desire the thing to know,—
" In garden placed, or in the wild,
With sunshine warm, or cold with snow?

" Where is that wondrous place?" he said,
"Of which mamma and you do talk;
Is it on high, above mine head,
Or where my striving feet may walk?

"The World, oh shall I see the place
When I a bigger boy am grown ?
And will it brighter make my face,
And will it sound with Music's tone ?"

" Dear dreaming child," the father said,
" Why should I break thy pleasant sleep.
Why sorrow wreathe about thine head,
Anent the World that's in the deep.

" And yet, oh boy, thou wilt not rest,
But question put for evermore,
Until that I have met thy quest,
And told where lies that mystic shore.

" The World, dear boy, as one hath said,
All in the Wicked One doth lie ;
Nor hath it glory on its head,
Nor sun, nor moon, nor starry sky.

" Deep in the Wicked One it dwells,
And dark and lonesome is the place ;
No birds rejoice, no music swells,
Where glooms its hard, inverted face.

" Deep in the Wicked One, oh boy,
It keepeth now and hideth aye ;
Believe me, boy, it hath no joy,
No breezy morn, no sunny day.

" Yet shall the World one day arise,
And to the Father sweetly go ;
With lowly heart and dewy eyes,
Shall cry the World in accents low,—

" 'Oh, Father throned in Heaven above,
I've wander'd far in lonely night,
And broke Thy holy law of love,
And quench'd within Thy glorious light.

" 'Oh Father, fold Thy wandering sheep,
Whom husks have fed upon the wild,
For gone is now my treacherous sleep;
Oh take me back, Thy long-lost child.'

"So shall the World be fair again,
And joy shall be upon its head,
When it upriseth from the plain,
And to the King of Glory's wed.

" Ah, then, dear boy, when older grown,
All freely thou shalt see the place,
No longer known as Mammon's throne,
But beauteous seen as angel's face."

A MORNING VISION.

"Sweep, sweep," he cried, with high, sonorous tone,
And sharply came the note along the wind:
I oped my casement ere the note was flown,
When met mine eye a dusky form inclined.

"Sweep, sweep," he cried, and peer'd on every side,
And seem'd importunate some work to find;
I looked, and saw the sable could not hide
The subtle workings of the kingly mind.

"Sweep, sweep," he cried, with calm and manly mien,
And shone the light of labour in his eye,
For saw he not his semblance dark, I ween,
But as the eagle soars did touch the sky.

"Sweep, sweep," he cried, with music all unknown,
Nor thought God's angels in the arching deep
Did joyous waft it to the burning throne
Of Him who notes our speech, nor waits to sleep.

"Sweep, sweep," he said, and now with plaintive cry,
And oh, my soul went forth his voice to greet;
I caught in symbol-tone the World's deep sigh,
As having lost since morn its golden seat.

"Sweep, sweep," he cried, again with voice sublime,
Dissolved his cloudy vestment in the light;
Came stealing down the air the Seraphs' chime,
I woke, and fled the vision from my sight.

THE MAGDALENE.

THE time was holy Christmas Eve,
The place vast Babel dimly seen,
When saw I what my lay doth weave,
And thrill'd with inward grief, I ween.

The air was chill, and dark the night,
And voiceless was the fitful wind ;
Red fog put out the gaseous light,
Yet busy strove the realm of mind.

Chanced it that eve, near midnight hour,
I pass'd athwart the teeming plain,
Whose house-tops dim that veil hung o'er,
As of its pomps in cold disdain.

Or may be, in more wrathful mood,
The gloomy sprite loom'd darkly there,
As seeing sever'd brotherhood,
As hearing revel more than prayer.

So heavy hung the blinding cloud,
While dance and song stirr'd life within ;
And merry voices shouted loud
In joy to lead young Christmas in.

Thus drear and dark was London now
In all its outward semblance found ;
While in bright rooms full wine-cups flow,
And music yields its witching sound.

I cross'd, as sung, this spreading field,
Where prickly thorns do thickly grow,
And Mammon doth hard sceptre wield,
And freeze the place with polar snow.

I cross'd the place with weary foot,
And more with sick and bleeding heart ;
And sorrow'd much that flower and fruit
Should only grow as things apart.

And wonder'd too within my soul,
Since cumber'd much the groaning ground,
How He who worketh for the whole
Should e'en as one who sleeps be found.

And so in bitterness I wept,
As death with life did struggle there ;
And up the night complaining swept
The utterance of a broken prayer.

"Oh, Holy One of quenchless love!
Oh, Beauteous One the Cross that bore!
Look from Thy glorious heights above,
And open Thou thy golden door.

"Behold in death this People lies,
In death it sleeps 'mid all its joy;
In death for aye it groans and sighs,
For in its mirth is woe's alloy.

"So look Thou down, oh, Kingly One!
And give it rest, as Thou canst do;
And bear it up before Thy throne,
And calm its mighty ebb and flow."

While yet this word was on my tongue,
And soar'd my thought the world beyond,
My soul anew with anguish wrung,
And woke desire with yearning fond;

.

I stood where flows the river's tide,
Near where the Abbey lifts its head;
I stood, for one was at my side
Who sought that tide with arms outspread.

A pale and troubled face I saw,
With brow where beauty linger'd still;
She seem'd to court that river's jaw,
As if therein to drown her ill.

A smother'd scorn, a stifled woe,
Did wrestle in her stormy eye,
As there she paced to and fro,
Uncertain or to flee or die.

With inmost grief she pierced my soul,
That stricken heart a-bleeding there ;
I sought her sorrow to control,
I sought it with a brother's prayer.

I thought of Him who bore our pain,
The Man of Sorrows inly known ;
I thought, too, of the world's disdain,
And that pale martyr sad and lone.

And so in broken words, I cried,
And bore her on my heart's deep love,
" O Christ the strong, Thy face not hide,
But send in haste the quickening dove,

" And let it nestle pure and warm
In this my sorrowing sister's soul,
And soothe with song this rending storm,
And make her once more glad and whole."

And as I pray'd I sought her arm,
And drew her from the fatal spot,
And heard her tale of shame and harm,
And saw the links that bound her lot.

Awhile ago, a virgin pure
As blushing morn, she oped the day ;
Anon pass'd by a treacherous wooer,
And quench'd in night the sunny ray.

Awhile ago, from towns afar,
And all their false and fever'd life,
She knew not much of Hate's stern war
As join'd to her who is not wife,

Yet as a wife doth yield her love
With tenderness no speech may tell,
But weepeth soon a bleeding dove,
Struck by a base and coward will.

She knew not this, being all unlearn'd
In arts which rend what God hath knit,
And so but little she discern'd
What in His Holy Book is writ :

How that the pure in heart are bless'd,
And they alone the Father see,
And dwell with Him in bowers of rest
Upholden by His Spirit free.

Her book of life is blurr'd and torn,
The book of death is writ in tears ;
She walks the earth a thing forlorn,
With woe consumed and smit with fears.

In mockery cold men call her gay,
" Unfortunate " they name her state ;
They leave her in the dark broad way,
All careless of her awful fate.

They slay her life where it doth spring
From depths of infinite desire ;
Toy they an hour, then spurn the thing,
And nothing leave but death's dark pyre.

Oh that my soul could utterance find
To tell the anguish of this hour,
I'd fly on stormy wings of wind
And bear the grief the wide world o'er.

I'd tell how Fashion, proud and cold,
Doth pompous gloat in glittering hall,
And steals the lamb from distant wold,
And heartless strikes, nor heeds the fall.

How Fashion, thirsting to be great,
In Hell's dark kingdom soon to pass,
Doth undermine the social state,
Yet fair is seen in darken'd glass.

For all things here are darkly seen,
A film doth hide the higher light,
And Fashion glories in the screen,
Nor dreams it walks alone in night.

But Fashion shall be slain ere long,
And vex no more this troubled life:
I see on high God's angels strong,
With trump in hand and gleaming knife.

God's angels strong do fill the sky,
Their loins girt up with awful might,
Before them thick the storm-clouds fly,
And all portends the coming night.

With sickle bright and keen they come,
The harvest of the Earth to reap,
The sheaves to bind and carry home,
The chaff with whirlwind far to sweep.

Before them rides in radiant car
One brighter far than sun at noon,
And looks He like a Man of war
With sword of vengeance coming soon.

So, Fashion, turn thee from thy pride,
Spurn not the outcast from thy door,
Sweet Mercy's gates throw open wide,
Avert the storm ere yet it pour.

So shalt thou, Fashion, be no more,
But tender human love be found,
So shalt thou sing for evermore,
And music breathe o'er all the ground.

WHERE I WAS BORN.

WHERE bloweth fresh the air on breezy down
And stirreth all the blood to quicker flow,
Where to the plough the glebe upturneth brown
And throbbeth to the sun with gentle glow:

Where in the dewy morn on lyric wing
The joyous lark upclimbs the azure dome,
And to the coming day sweet songs doth sing,
Rejoicing evermore in that high home:

Where in the stilly eve athwart the wold
The sheep-bell tinkles in the fading light,
And Fancy wakes with pleasant dreams of old
As blends the cheery sound with silent night:

Where through the laughing day from Spring to Spring
The rustic tills the soil as they afore,
And to the airy fields doth steadfast cling,
And to the rose that climbs his sacred door:

Where in the village street that Freedom loves,
What time the corn is golden in the grain,
With pleasant rural sound all stately moves
The harvest of the year in loaded wain :

Where from the spacious barn that keeps the sheaves,
When Winter sleeps in all the drowsy fields,
The thrasher's flail doth woo the list'ning eaves,
And charmeth those who hear and him who wields:

Where spreading elms do bind the hamlet round,
And shady lanes lead up to where it shows,
And rolls a babbling brook with merry sound,
And orchards shed in Spring fair blooms and snows:

Where at the back, athwart the rippling rill,
Green lines of hawthorn block the noisy world,
And immemorial stiles where lovers thrill
Are seen with leafy branches o'er them curl'd :

Where evermore, as fly the hours away,
And cross the bourne from whence they ne'er return,
Fair Nature rules the place with mighty sway,
And high above the Cherubs' Sword doth turn :

Where in the wolds a charming walk withdrawn
Great Alfred's ancient town salutes the sky,
With well whereto the pilgrim's foot is drawn
By love led forth to greet it with a sigh.

There on a day some forty suns ago,
As fond tradition says, awoke the bard
Who here in peaceful numbers soft and low
High Art doth gently woo for Art's reward.

There from the inner Heavens beyond the sun,
Where budding souls on angel-breasts recline,
An infant came I down my course to run,
While o'er me sweetly watched the Muses nine.

There in an ancient house, which long had borne
The storms of wind and flood adown the years,
Came I upon the dewy wings of morn,
And welcomed was with laughter and with tears.

There saw I first the light of earthly day,
And took the place where Love had set my bound ;
There 'gan the struggles of life's tragic way ;
There knew I first the groaning of the ground.

There by the wondrous gates of sight and sound
The flow of Space and Time my soul did find;
There lay I mute in all the vocal round,
Till from its slumber woke the kingly mind.

There first the charm of speech broke on mine ear,
And heard I Love in human accents sweet,
And saw I mingle, too, high Beauty's tear,
And long'd to rise and kiss the gracious feet.

There lisp'd I first with slow and stammering tongue
That holy name of love which Love reveal'd;
And round about my mother's knees I clung,
As now the lips of silence were unseal'd.

There in that still, reposeful house I woke,
And pass'd the years of Childhood's golden prime
The World afar and all its galling yoke,
A mystic dream and song that golden time.

There, nurtured by the breezes of the down,
My life upgrew, though feeble was the frame;
There mighty freedom as a seed was sown,
And loved I more and more its glorious name.

There in that restful spot I saw the day,
There sported with the flowers upon the lea,
There love I still bright Summer's fragrant hay,—
There would I rest when that I've cross'd the Sea.

ASPROMONTE.

O THOU, Italia's Star, that glancing with swift ray
For some brief hours hath cheer'd her lone and stormy
    night,
And led with fiery hand and grand heroic soul
Her pale and bleeding sons o'er mountains dark and cold
Her dastard foes to smite with Love's resistless brand,
And scatter'd them as chaff before the wind is hurl'd;
Who, like great Joshua of the fervid Hebrew Race,
That erst with feeble bands, and, scorn'd, did swiftly
    quench
By arm of God the lust and hate of Canaan's hosts,
And built the realm of Truth and Right for all the World,
Hath now in this tempestuous Age to Chaos nigh
With followers few, yet nerved as they with strength
    sublime,
Dread Freedom's holy banner raised afore the sky,
And by the whisper'd terror of thy glorious name
Hath blanch'd the tyrant's cheek and broke his rest
    afar ;—

Thou, in whose burning eye the light of other sun
Than this dull orb with bright electric ray doth gleam,
Who'st sent abroad the thrilling word that Death must
    die,
And loose the cords which long our stricken race have
    bound,
And set thy brothers free, at will to greet the day;
Ill Fame doth say of thee, thou beauteous Star of Eve,
That Destiny's fell hand hath pluck'd thee from thy seat
In arc of Heaven, and cast thee down to this cold earth,
And mingled thee as man of common mould with men.
The same detracting tongue doth likewise noise abroad
That thou who'st loosen'd bitter bonds art bound thyself,
That thou who'st heal'd heart wounds art wounded in
    thy soul,
That friends of thine own House thy path have com-
    pass'd round,
And check'd thy high career, and roll'd thy flag in dust,
And set thy poor Italia's sons to weep as oft before,
And thee do hold as one his steps forbid to choose,
With not a foot of soil thine own in all that land.—
But can it be, sweet mournful Star, Italia's Child,
That thou from that unfathom'd blue art fallen here?
Ah, no, the night is wreath'd with mist, Earth's eye is
    dim,
And so thy shining is not seen, nor felt thy ray ;
But soon, methinks too soon, the straining sight the vault
Will search, and yearn to know that calm thou shinest
    there,

For signs of tempest dire and dark do stir the air,
And flicker down in all the light and robe the cloud,
And mingle solemn whisperings with the moaning wind;
The eagles, too, do gather fast and fill the sky.
Ah, well, Italia in that hour with anguish fill'd
That soon will press thee sore and spoil thy treacherous
       sleep,
Thrice well if he who now lies bound and crush'd for thee
May rise as from thy dead, and, like strong Samson girt
With highest might when as was thought most weak
       and lone,
Wrap close in death the hosts which thy great hope
       would slay.

'AN ODE TO THE VIRGIN.

HAIL, Mary, thou of women bless'd ;
E'en thou with brightest glory crown'd ;
My soul hath long thy grace confess'd,
And in thy presence sweetness found.

With thee I've trod Judæa's hills,
And drank the music of its streams ;
And with thy form my memory thrills,
With thee I wander still in dreams.

I see thee as thou walkedst then,
When bow'd the Heavens, and sojourn'd there ;
On wavy plain, in mountain glen,
A beauteous virgin clad in prayer.

The Graces blent thy form to build,
The Muses wrapt thee close with song ;
All peerless in Love's mighty guild,
Thou chiefest art in all the throng.

Hail, Mary, thou of women bless'd,
Whose is the one-begotten Son ;
My soul hath e'er thy love confess'd,
And join'd thee in thine orison.

With thee I've sung from heart of love
The song that breathes His glorious Name ;
With thee on golden wings I move,
Oft as awakes its sacred flame.

Thy Lord and mine with thee I sing,
In love come down to save the Race,
With gifts of healing in His wing,
And radiant beauty in His face.

Thy blushing lowliness I greet,
And all thy tender virgin thought ;
I bow me gently at thy feet,
And pomp of Earth do count as nought.

With ages long I count thee bless'd,
And in thee joy as lifted high
My soul hath long thy might confess'd,
Exalted in a cloudless sky.

With thee I laud His mercy shown
On them for aye who fear His Name ;
With thee confess His mighty throne,
Wherefrom proceeds the burning flame,

From whose pure heat the proud retire,
And eke the mighty quail in fear,
As not akin to holy fire,
But knit to Earthly matter here.

With thee I note the hungry fill'd
With living bread and generous wine,
While all the rich whom love ne'er thrill'd
Are sent away without a sign.

With thee I note His promise kept
Which He afore to Israel swore,
Though long to outward sense it slept,
But now with blessing brimmeth o'er.

With thee high glory e'er I yield
To Father, Son, and Spirit one ;
For aye in all the starry field
The song shall flow in unison.

Hail, Mary, thou of women bless'd,
I greet thee with my heart's deep love ;
My soul hath long thy grace confess'd,
And soon will see thy face above.

"WHEN I AWAKE."

WHEN in thy likeness dear, oh, beauteous One!
At Resurrection Morn my soul shall wake,
And see Thee calm and fair on golden throne,
And Thou shalt own me for sweet Mercy's sake:

When clad in flowing robes Thou then shalt give,
My soul shall wingèd move as doth the light,
And in thy conscious Presence ever live,
Nor fear again the coming of the night :

When taint of sin shall vex the life no more,
But pure and holy shall be all the blood,
And thy long banish'd ones shall tread the shore
That radiant shines afar athwart the flood:

When once again the blurr'd and broken race,
Long wandering on the mountains dark and cold,
Shall all convergent be to Thy blest face,
And all the sheep shall make one only fold ;

When Time's dark waves shall cease their striving flow,
Loud breaking on a stern and barren strand ;
When Space shall hide no more where Thou dost go
With spreading mantle in a shadowy land :

Oh then, when shall my soul from sleep awake,
And darksome dreams no more shall break its rest,
When with thy saints I dwell by placid lake,
And sinks the sun no more below the west.

Oh then, when in Thy boundless Heavens I wake,
A seed in weakness sown, but raised in might,
And on my soul Thy holy likeness take,
High God of God ! Eternal Light of Light !

Oh then, when seeing Thee e'en as Thou art,
And knowing as mine inmost soul is known,
Deep tides of joy shall fill my restful heart,
E'en then when I awake before thy Throne.

Yes, then, when wakes my soul like unto Thee—
To Thee, the glorious King of Truth and Love ;
Oh then shall blinding Sorrow swiftly flee,
And in my breast shall sing the gentle dove.

Oh then, when I awake in likeness Thine,
And know my former sinful self no more ;
Ah then, sweet Christ ! with Thee I'll drink the wine—
Bright ruby wine—upon the golden shore.

THE KING OF GLORY.

High Glory's King art Thou, O Christ, for aye !
My soul confesses none but only Thee ;
Or here below, or 'yond the realm of day,
Thee, Thee I seek in every land and sea.

High Glory's King art Thou, O Christ, the strong !
My soul Thy might hath found in Sorrow's gloom :
My feeble steps Thy love hath aided long,
And Thou shalt bear me up beyond the tomb.

High Glory's King art Thou, O Christ, the true !
Thy faithfulness I've known thro' all the night ;
Thou show'st me what to seek, and what eschew.
And clothest Thou my soul in robes of light.

High Glory's King art Thou, O Christ, the fair !
In all the starry dome there's none like Thee ;
Thou'rt Light in light, and fragrance in the air,
Thou'rt beauty in the flower that decks the lea.

High Glory's King art Thou, O Christ, the young!
And giftest Thou thy saints in youth to grow,
To speak again with childhood's guileless tongue,
And lilies cull where stilly waters flow.

High Glory's King art Thou, O Christ, great knight!
Thou coverest mine head in battle's hour,
When faint and low Thou girdest me for fight,
And crownest me with joy when battle's o'er.

High Glory's King art Thou, Thou first and last,
Afore the birth of Morn—dim Eve beyond,
Thou bringest golden corn from out the waste,
And bindest all the sheaves with Love's sweet bond.

High Glory's King art Thou from age to age,
Thy saints know only Thee adown the years;
High Priest for aye, and Holy Prophet sage,
They follow Thee, borne high beyond their fears.

High Glory's King art Thou, O Christ, dear Love!
Of myrrh thy garments smell and cassia sweet;
With Thee in dewy meads thy children rove,
And by calm waters sit afore thy feet.

High Glory's King art Thou, dear Lamb of God!
Thou bear'st our weary sin as though thine own,
Fell hate doth smite Thee with th' oppressor's rod.
Yet liftest Thou the Race to share thy Throne.

MY SHEPHERD.

THE kingly Christ my Shepherd is for aye,
What needs my restful soul when He is near ?
In pastures green He feeds me all the day,
And by the stilly waters charms mine ear.

When wounded is my soul with sin and shame,
And deep in Sorrow's darksome sea I move,
Oh then I hear the music of His Name !
Oh then once more I taste His righteous love.

Nor will I know or gloomy doubt or fear,
Though through the shadowy vale of death I walk ;
For Thou, dear Christ, art with me all the year,
And on Thy staff I lean, and hear Thee talk.

And when, as though, sweet Love, Thou wert afar,
My foes with sweep of flood burst on my soul,
Thou bearest me on high, from star to star,
And all is song and feast from pole to pole.

For with the soft and mystic oil of love
Thou dost afore them all mine head anoint,
And from Thy golden cup, in Heaven above,
Thou pourest joy through every weary joint.

And knoweth well my soul, dear bounteous Lord,
Thy grace and love shall dwell with me for aye ;
And in the glorious temple of thy Word
All sweetly shall I spend immortal day.

ASPIRATION.

As pants the hart when doth the Dog-star burn,
In water-brooks to cool his fever'd tongue ;
E'en so my thirsting soul to God doth turn,
And crieth out for Him with anguish wrung.

For hath my soul with bitter tears been fed,
Both day and night when hath Thy face been hid :
While mocking ask my foes where I am led,
And where art Thou, my God, and why I'm chid.

But doth sweet Memory yield again the times,
When festal clad unto thine House I went ;
And joyful voices blent with Music's chimes,
And wingèd praises up the azure sent.

And calling thus to mind these hallowed hours,
My soul is pourèd out from deep to deep ;
Nor can I roam the fields and cull the flowers,
Nor taste as then the sweets of balmy sleep.

Yet why, my fainting soul, art thou cast down,
Why troubled thus are all thine inner springs?
The Face which seemeth now to wear a frown
Shall shine again—and shalt thou mount on wings.

But is my soul, O God, cast down to-night,
Nor hath it power to rise and touch thy feet:
Yet shall great Jordan pass before my sight,
And Mizar's hill—for is their memory sweet.

Deep calleth unto deep within my soul,
As roll thy waves, O God, with awful roar;
And all is drear and dark from pole to pole,
And am I stricken down, I cannot soar.

Yet, Lord, art Thou for aye a loving Lord,
And wilt Thou crown the day once more with love,
And give me in the night a lyric word,
And lift me up in prayer to Thee above.

So will I search, O God, and inly know
Why Thou dost hide when most my foes do rage,
And all my bones are rent with grief and woe,
I'll learn of Thee why they this war do wage.

Why then, O soul, thus vexed and torn to-day,
Because they mocking say, where's now thy God?
Thou yet to Him shalt raise the tuneful lay,
And shall He soothe thee with His staff and rod.

PRAISE.

PRAISE waits for Thee, O God, on Zion's hill,
To Thee shall every soul sweet offering make ;
O Thou who hearest prayer with loving will,
With love of Thee shall all the world awake.

And though through weakness of the tempted flesh
Our sins have bound us in dim Sorrow's hour;
Yet Thou from chaff thy precious wheat shalt thresh,
And fan in hand shalt cleanse Thy cumber'd floor.

And blest, indeed, is he whom Thou dost choose,
And drawest to Thy feet Thy Courts within ;
Who kept by Thee doth ne'er their fragrance lose,
But resteth there as in sweet home akin.

For there in righteous judgment art Thou known,
And dost Thou strength afford all mixed with fear :
O Thou, the hope of all from zone to zone,
On sea afar, or home and kindred near.

Who by Thy strength dost hold the hills in rest
And calmest all the roaring of the sea,
And when the People move in stormy west
Dost still them with an inward melody.

The tokens of Thy power are known afar,
And fear of Thee is waken'd all around,
Thou risest sweet and fair, the morning Star,
And glory of the gentle eve art found.

The parchèd earth with rain dost Thou revive,
And with Thy dew doth keep it rich and fair,
And causest Thou the golden corn to thrive
When temper'd sweetly is the nurturing air.

For Thou it is who doth the water pour
On all the ridges of the glebe upturn'd,
And softenest Thou the soil with cooling shower
When hath the scorching sun too hotly burn'd.

So dost Thou bless the springing of the grain
And all the fruitful year with goodness crown,
And do Thy paths drop fatness on the plain,
And from the wild take all its dreary frown.

And do the hills rejoice because of Thee,
While bleating flocks the smiling pastures grace,
And corn-fill'd valleys dance with sportive glee,
And all things own the beauty of Thy Face.

"FAINT YET PURSUING."

FAINTETH, O Lord, my soul to-night,
For grief hath bruised me all the day,
In vain I struggle to the light,
I cannot reach the quickening ray.

Faint must I wholly be for aye
Unless Thou holdest up my feet
And goest with me in the way,
The darksome way of Satan's seat.

Faint Thou dear Christ, the World and I,
We faint beneath a torrid sun ;
Oh, give us wings to touch the sky
And pæans sing for victory won.

Faint are we through the weary year,
The whole Creation groans in pain,
And darkness lies on all the sphere
Until that Thou be come again.

Faint are the ages, Lord of Might,
High Glory's King for evermore,
Faint have they long been all the night,
When shall Thy feet be on the shore ?

Thy shining feet where Music dwells,
Where Mary knelt in prayer and song,
Where tears are pour'd when Passion swells,
How long, dear feet, how long, how long ?

And yet though faint the World and I,
And sleeps the Church a deadly sleep,
We climb the heights when Thou art nigh
And fearless tread the stormy deep.

Though faint and weak pursuing still
When sounds Thy voice upon the wave,
And is Thy footstep on the hill,
For Thou we know hast oped the grave.

If faint are we yet Thou art strong,
And loving too and gracious e'er ;
Pursue we then—stay not Thou long,
We wait to see Thee in the air.

If faint and low at midnight hour,
When all the stars with mist are dim,
And cometh not refreshing shower,
O world ! O soul ! let's wait for Him,—

For Him, dear Christ, the strong and true,
Whose chariot wheels I hear, I hear,
Uprise we then and still pursue,
The rosy morning now is near.

The morning without clouds doth come,
I see it rising in the East,
Oh, soon we'll rest in peace at home
With lyric song at marriage-feast.

III.

CUM RISÛ.

AN ODE TO SMOKERS.

DEAR patrons of great Raleigh's fragrant weed,
Sweet subjects of the limping god of fire,
With whom to smoke is hope, and life, and creed,
Transcendent gift sent on to son from sire :

With whom to smoke is honey'd sweet to find,
Ere morn hath clomb as yet the kindling East,
Nor food less fair of high ambrosial kind,
When drowsy are the eyes of man and beast :

With whom to smoke, throughout the flying day,
And pour strange incense on the wondering air,
Is e'er to bask in Pleasure's sunniest ray,
And breathe, in typic way, the smoker's prayer.

To you, the salamanders of the world,
Strong fire-souls, floating on a flaming sea,—
To you my fluttering banner is unfurl'd,
To you it gently waves with motion free.

To you my song ascends, with tremulous wing,
Through mist and gloom it struggles up the dome ;
For yearns it much on that high sea to sing,
And sound aloud the joys of that far home.

Strives it to catch the placid tone and air
Of joyous spirits sporting there on high,
To represent the " ubi gentium " where
That fiery sea doth roll in upper sky.

Oh, longs the Muse to weave for days to come,
In flowing numbers soft, and sweet, and low,
An " in memoriam " lay of that bright home,
Where sprites so bless'd do ceaseless come and go.

There poets are, who sing of war and love,
Of knights and ladies fair, in times gone by ;
How those the right to guard the world did rove,
How these did lure them on with smile and sigh.

But times are changed, and changed the ways of men,
And even poets take this mortal form ;
And prosy things do utter now and then,
And learnedly discourse of cloud and storm.

So quits my Muse the grand ideal sphere,
And cometh down to things of smell and taste ;
Yet moves she still with blithe and hearty cheer,
And bids dull mourners quit the dreary waste.

The lofty joys of sense be all my song,—
Of sense as known on that high sea of flame—
Of sense most exquisitely sweet and strong :
To this I give in verse a deathless name.

Vain speculative men do roam about,
And idly seek where dwells the chiefest good ;
Their tortured brains they beat to find it out,
Not seen, it hidden lies in this high food.

Not seen, though some do see it clear and plain,
Who note the radiant airs which fire-sprites show ;
Who read in all their brow the glorious gain,
And see how great and fair they seem to grow.

The chiefest good I sing it here to-day,
In cloudy incense filling all the air,
The chiefest good I give it current way,
And bid it henceforth travel everywhere.

Yet e'en the chiefest good is under law,
The chiefest good as known to mortals here ;
For is it held a wise and ancient saw—
This good to some is far, to others near.

For every good doth all its aspect take,
Accordant with the light in which it's seen ;
And so doth many forms and fashions make
As is the eye, or blue, or grey, or green.

For good, though in its glorious essence one,
Unchangeable for aye from age to age ;
Outliving evermore or star or sun,
And bound with golden links to saint and sage.

Yet, in its passage through the realms of sense,
Of erring sense a broken mirror found,
Doth come refracted through the shatter'd lens,
And often takes the colour of the ground.

And thus it is, that what is meat to one,
And swells the crimson tide with flowing life,
In other veins doth acrid poison run,
And carry with it only deadly strife.

E'en so, the salamander's flamy good,
Outflowing evermore on that high sea,
Although to those akin etherial food,
Now sporting there, now sweeping all the lea.

Yet may it be to men of earthlier mould,
Whose solid frames are built of common clay ;
E'en as a nuisance vast (how great untold),
A nuisance killing all the fragrant day.

For these compacted of the earthy soil,
Who love the scents which fill the flowery vale ;
Where suck the " busy bees " with dainty toil,
And smokers shun as they themselves the gale.

AN ODE TO SMOKERS.

No gift possess of immemorial birth,
Downcoming 'long the great ancestral line ;
That tends to show their transcendental worth,
Or to the realm of fire doth them assign.

Along the Queen's highway they humbly move,
And ample curves describe where fire-sprites pass,
And yearn to fly afar on wings of dove,
And sigh to know they are but withering grass.

No power have they to drink the smoky flame,
No sense its fragrant incense to perceive :
And so they dwell alone with night and shame,
And if to smoke constrained but make believe.

And if perchance of these the baser sort,
Who are not framed to thrive on fire and smoke,
Some daring soul should with fire-forms resort,
And think that eating fire is all a joke ;

And wed the alien incense to his soul,
And dream to float upon the fiery wave,
And pass the narrow bounds of Earth's control,
And taste Elysian bliss that owns no grave ;

Alas ! full soon he's given to know and feel
What 'tis one's native element to quit,
For now with sickly qualms he 'gins to reel,
Nor findeth he in ease to stand or sit.

Gone is the splendid fabric of his dream,
And knows he now how earthy is his frame;
No more shall he aspire with fire to gleam,
Nor madly hope to win the smoker's fame.

Full well he's learnt that good is not the same,
To diverse natures mix'd in differing form;
And evermore he shuns that specious flame,
Nor courts what is to him a drowning storm.

But other some there are of this weak frame,
Who know themselves to be of earth compact,
And ne'er do venture out to wed with flame,
But ever have forsworn that doubtful act.

For these, O ye etherial spirits strong,
For these I plead, albeit with faltering strain,
Your chiefest good yourselves to keep among,
And mingle not your pleasure with their pain.

For these I seek, with lyric song and prayer,
You'd eat your fire like other food at home,
Nor pour it any more in all the air,
On sea or land wherever men do roam.

And most of all for their poor sakes I ask,
Your chiefest good you'd not so oft obtrude,
As by the rail you daily seek the task
Of head or hand which lifts you from the rude.

But hold the same for the domestic hearth,
And share it there with spirits like yourselves;
There may ye sip its sweets, in joy and mirth,
There take your fill for aye as flaming elves.

•

THE LONDON CARTER;

OR, "THE REASON WHY."

ON London bridge in London town,
What time red fog did hide the sky,
Mine eye perceived a civic clown
Intent to solve "the reason why."

A thing of Herculean build,
And staunch and bold as he was huge ;
A lineal shoot from Bashan's guild,
He clearly scorn'd all subterfuge.

A ponderous wain was at his heel,
A vast and ponderous horse before ;
While high in air the common weal
Of merchant stuff was flowing o'er.

Adown the sides and at the tail,
And eke in front where he should sit,
The mighty pile rose, bale on bale,
And harshly on his seat had lit.

And now upon this crowded bridge,
This bridge of equal noise and dirt ;
His problem was to clear the ridge,
And eke to save his failing shirt.

To clear the ridge that would not move,
To save the shirt that would dissolve,
He called as one afore on Jove
The point to show how to resolve.

But selfish Jove, as then so now,
Intent on things that bear no toil,
But left him swearing in the slough
And sweating in the grimy soil.

I paused as I had done afore,
And look'd with wonder on the scene ;
There were the bales all flowing o'er,
There was the wain where it had been.

But he, the carter, standing there,
And waiting for the mass to move,
The mass far reaching up the air
That would not take the facile groove ;

He clearly was a man of wit,
If somewhat stolid in its kind ;
And all at once his brow was lit,
And all at once shot out his mind.

With solid Saxon weight it came,
And swell'd his frame before its might ;
While in his face it lit a flame,
Not all of day, nor all of night.

And now as waxes broad the Moon
From crescent line to rounded form,
So had my rapturous wonder grown
To see the rising of the storm.

But now, as one in times of old,
A certain Greek, his name forgot,
Said proudly that he'd move the world
If but a fulcrum he had got :

E'en so this ponderous man of wit,
Deep musing here of cause and law,
Reflected how in books 'twas writ
And current was " an ancient saw ; "

That e'en as love doth kindle love
So like doth always like beget,
Which gathering from some mental grove,
He now applieth without let.

'Tis motion that his soul doth need,
And motion he's resolved to get,
And so with lightning's force and speed
Each muscle of his frame is set ;

Is set, is set for one sole end,
To wield a whip of mighty size ;
With potent might to cut and rend,
And clear his way (for he is wise).

The whip I saw high poised in air,
The shirt was hotter than before ;
His eyes shot out a lurid glare,
He storm'd and shouted more and more:

And inarticulate voice he found,
All husky too, in carter's way ;
Loud boom'd and thick the thudding sound,
" Gee-up, wooaa! gee-up ! I say."

" Gee-up !" he cried, both loud and deep,
" Gee-up, wooaa ! thou stubborn beast ; "
The whip, too, strove to break the sleep,
Yet could not shake the sleeper's rest.

Inert, insensate not he stood,
Firm " locking up " the groaning road,
While sterner grew the carter's mood,
And louder crack'd the whip abroad.

So there they stood, the horse and man,
There stood the wain upon the bridge ;
Let him them move who move them can,
And get them o'er that mighty ridge.

I wot they'd stood for ever there
But for a social brotherhood,
That will not let big carters swear
Against dumb beasts, nor draw their blood ;

That will not have that carter's whip
Go thwacking on the poor thing's back ;
Keen searching him from head to hip,
With three times three loud whack on whack.

So now there came another beast,
More ponderous still than he in wain,
When gleam'd the sun from out the East,
Through all the fog to see the same.

The sun peep'd forth, the horse hitch'd on,
And slowly crept the wain again ;
The carter's face it dimly shone,
As now he plodded in the " main."

And much I wonder'd in my soul,
Why law of motion shouldn't be fed,
And gravitation should control
Alike the wain and eke the head.

And ponder'd much the ponderous thing,
And turn'd it long within my thought,
Why carters could not furnish wing,
Whereby sweet motion might be wrought.

To me it seem'd a problem small,
All lying close within a shell
Of filbert, or of peach on wall,
To draw the waggon from the dell.

For, though high cause wise men forswear,
In this great age of smoky light,
And all things make to flow in air,
With nought to give them going might;

And view the glorious tidal flow
Of this deep World as sequence dumb,
And freeze its life in arctic snow,
And mete the whole by rule of thumb;

Though see they not with inward eye
The mighty Will that underlies
All motion known below—on high,
In earth and sea, and boundless skies.

Yet motion waits on mind alone,
As erst from mind it swept abroad,
And wingèd cross'd the starry zone,
With sound of harp along the road.

But mind, which motion is to all,
Is that which fail'd that carter there;
And so he stood in helpless thrall,
And little did he more than swear.

"The reason why, the reason why,"
He could not get the wain to go,
Was more than glanced within his eye,
He could not solve the problem so.

Nor were his masters wiser found,
The cotton lords of this great age ;
They, too, the thread had not unwound,
Though "up in stuffs," in prices sage.

For had they known high motion's law,
Obedient e'er to flow of mind ;
They'd seen what I most clearly saw,
How lagg'd the wain from weight behind.

From weight behind the horse's back,
And nothing else, the waggon stuck ;
Not seen through stint of brain alack,
And so the light was never struck.

Like high philosophers of mind,
Of mind to-day as dimly known,
The carter and his lords inclined
To get the "go" by force alone.

By brutal force of oath and whip,
And meltings of the failing shirt,
By flogging well the dumb thing's hip,
They thought the wain to drag from dirt.

Alas! they shut their eyes to this,
That brutal force all mind doth stop;
So "vis inertiæ" made them miss,
And all their high pretensions drop.

So carters of the whip and shop,
A moral draw from this poor lay;
Whene'er a wain in rut doth stop,
Let mind arise and clear the way.

"NIL ADMIRARI."

"THANKS," quoth egotistic Fashion, t'other day,
For some poor favour one had coldly shown ;
"Thanks," no kindly breath is in me more to say,
For you and I are two, but I am one.

"Thanks," good sir, and will not that meet all your
       thought,
And are not all agreed to be thus brief?
"Thanks," let all men now-a-days be curtly taught
That more than this to say is Fashion's grief.

"Thanks," I may not utter more, dear Fashion saith,
The Age forbids to say " I thank you, Sir ; "
"Thanks," oh, will not that content all fervid faith ?
Why put in I and you with so much stir ?

"Thanks," what, know you not "Nil Admirari's" here ?
And evermore doth hold the World in chains ;
"Thanks,"—oh, doubting Sir, you'll get no better cheer.
So pray yourself resign and save your pains.

"Thanks," I say, nor will I henceforth utter more,
 "Nil Admirari" hath no more to say ;
"Thanks,"—I charge you stop at that on sea or shore,
To say "I thank you" is no more the way.

"Thanks," quoth dainty Fashion, reasoning deep and
The mode is now, "Nil admirari 's" come ;   [well.
"Thanks," for it is short for those who buy and sell,
And as to you, why keep yourself at home.

"Thanks," no more for highest art, with toil achieved,
By those who burn the midnight oil in love ;
"Thanks," no more can now be thought of or believed,
Though I and you are knit in Heaven above.

"Thanks,"—oh, thinker, striving in the night of Time,
If e'er thou gettest barely this rejoice ;
"Thanks," "Nil admirari" cannot higher climb,
His heart, besides, is cold, and poor his voice.

"Thanks," the dying World is passing to the End,
And Fashion only shows the crisis near ;
"Thanks," oh, mighty God, thy forkèd lightning send,
And pour thy vengeance down on all the sphere.

"Thanks,"—take back the wretched sneer, thou grovel-
"Nil Admirari" owns no royal birth ;   [ling world,
"Thanks," I see on high Truth's banner fair unfurl'd,
And scorn thy low-born heritage of Earth.

"TENNYSON IS TENNYSON."

"TENNYSON is Tennyson," Time's oracle did say,
And eke the dictum gave quite in judicial way;
As sentence it would seem, deep reason'd from the root,
And hap'ly welded, too, with every notion moot.

"Tennyson is Tennyson as a is a," it said,
And much I wonder'd how with Euclid he should wed;
For a is a as measured quantum, fix'd and known,
And cut as pole from pole from man's ascending zone.

So mused I much and long, with vex'd and struggling
     thought,
And with that critic bold with flaming brand I fought,
Resolved with mighty Mars upholding mine advance,
That word from Chaos sprung to slay at point of lance.

"Tennyson is Tennyson,"—to say no more than this
Is only to betray with traitor's ghastly kiss,
For deeper read, the law can ne'er solution find,
Save as the Sense is pierced, and reach'd the realm of
     Mind.

When Tennyson is Tennyson no doubt sweet music flows,
While vanish all our mists, and perish all our snows,
And for the nonce we rise from hum of marts afar,
And mingle in the lists where strives a nobler war.

When Tennyson *seems* Tennyson, oh, then the music's
    flown,
And back the darkness comes with all the frozen zone,
And so once more we sink in dullness and despair,
And wonder much how late we soarèd in the air.

Let Tennyson *be* Tennyson, in altitude of song,
And take us up the heights where lyric angels throng ;
Oh, then with him we 'll drink the pulsing waves of sound,
And scorn the narrow cares which hold us to the ground.

Let Tennyson *be* Tennyson, and ne'er shall we complain,
As one who pleasure seeks, but findeth not the gain ;
Let Tennyson *seem* Tennyson, then all our ardour fades,
We seek, but find him not, we lose him in the shades.

Oh, Tennyson *be* Tennyson, thyself as thou canst be,
And at thy magic touch our sorrows all shall flee,
So climb thee with thy lyre to Love's bright realm of day,
And give us back in gushing strain a deathless lay.

"WHEN THOU DOEST WELL."

Oh, when thou doest well, dear Man,
E'en when thou sweetly doest well,
Ah, then soft breezes shall thee fan,
And will the World thy praises tell.

When favour'd by the breath of Fame,
Who blows her trumpet much at will,
Thou gettest to thyself a name,
And art no more a doubtful rill;

But swelling river sudden grown,
Of water broad, if scarcely deep,
And flowest by thyself alone,
And hastest much to climb the steep;

And passing in thy glorious flow,
The brooks which babble on the plain,
Doth lofty glances on them throw,
As thou dost travel to the main:

E'en now, when through the wondering lands,
Where do thy growing waters reach,
Thou showest fair with golden sands,
Mute symbols of a gracious speech :

E'en now, when is thy current strong,
And fed thy stream by rills pass'd by ;
And lauded is thy name in song,
And borne on breezes to the sky :

E'en now, when showeth fair thy form
As floats the cloud above thy face,
Nor fearest thou or wind or storm,
But is thy course one splendid race :

E'en now, when broken are thy banks,
Too stint and low for rushing stream ;
Now shall thy course be hail'd with thanks,
And shall thy wave with glory gleam.

Now shall the World and thee rejoice,
And shall thy banks be wider spread ;
And thou shalt find a louder voice,
Yet shalt thou not awake the dead.

Well hast thou done, broad-flowing stream.
Thou'st riches gathered in thy flow ;
But hast thou left the World to dream,
Nor helped it in its awful woe.

Well hast thou done, far-spreading stream,
All proudly didst thou break thy banks ;
Nor knew'st thy fame was idle dream,
While hollow were the sounding thanks ;

The sounding thanks which hail'd thy flow
And swell'd thy stream with turbid rain ;
They only show where thou dost go,
They only tend thee on the plain.

Yet in thy way thou doest well,
And spreading art, though scarcely deep ;
For this men do thy praises swell,
And what they sow they also reap.

But comes anon reflective day—
Flow back thou stream upon thy springs ;
For was thy course factitious way,
And lost art thou with dying things.

Flow back, poor stream, or deeper flow,
The World doth need the living tide ;
Far going where deep Oceans go,
Ascending where rapt Cherubs ride.

AN ODE TO "THE READER."

Oh, reader, have you read " The Reader,"
That calm yet mighty interpleader ;
And seen how high-souled Truth doth lead her.
And with the higher manna feed her ?

Oh, did you note her fair adorning,
When forth she came where springs the morning ;
With trumpet glorious things out-telling,
From ethic depths e'er upward welling ?

Oh, did you mark the happy seeming,
With stifled tear on eyelash gleaming,
That clad her in her late uprising,
When stole she on us all surprising ?

Her sweet and high and candid seeming,
Preferring truth, pure good esteeming ;
And critic's bâton nobly wielding,
And lofty Art intensely shielding ?

Say, did you not begin believing,
Sour critics o'er their spleen were grieving?
And henceforth would, all else forsaking,
Work only for the World's awaking?

E'en such I ween that outward seeming,
With much besides that left to gleaning;
Yet was that light naught but the gloaming,
And in its haze the sprite is roaming.

But now, to make this fact apparent,
Accept, dear reader, this my warrant;
The which I base on its endeavour,
When dark and dull, to seem quite clever.

The time was ere the leaf was green, O,
And fight was made about Colenso;
And all things seem'd to wreck agoing,
And critics were with wit o'erflowing.

With brilliant wit, electric glancing,
Sat they on lofty horses prancing;
The awful sword of justice wielding,
To all that's false and mean unyielding.

When thus was seen their gallant bearing,
What time Colenso was a-swearing
That sacred Writ was old wives' fable,
And nothing there was sure or stable.

Chanced it that now your humble servant,
The lists did enter, all observant ;
And met the foeman, nothing fearing,
And sought to get a calmer hearing.

And show'd the fight was all mistaken,
For that *the Book* was quite forsaken ;
And ne'er once came into the issue,
And what was spun mere cobweb tissue.

And as the ground of his endeavour,
Not being, like "The Reader," clever ;
He put it that "a voice" had won him,
Bright and incisive as the sun-beam.

And led him straight athwart the river,
That floweth deep and silent ever,
Between the World in outer seeming,
And the rapt spirits inner dreaming.

Feign'd he to stand where stood pale Cæsar,
What time he proved the World's great teazer :
To stand with him long inly musing,
To cross or not, where all's confusing.

Feign'd he that while he stood thus fearing,
And all seem'd dark and strange anear him ;
And rapid flew the mystic water,
Nor utter'd what might come hereafter.

This inner " voice" awoke with singing,
A mighty power with it bringing,
And bade him cross and march e'er sunward,
With banner writ "for ever onward."

Said he, moreo'er, the " voice" came sounding,
E'en as a lingering echo bounding,
That highly born when Time was olden
Still kept the air as something golden.

Still floated on the wings of morning,
Still grandly broke the shafts of scorning ;
An echo sprung from voice eternal,
And caught by earth "*en route*" diurnal.

An echo thrilling startled billow
What time great Moses show'd the hollow,
And Israel march'd 'twixt watery mountains,
And rose the sea erect like fountains.

Said he, this echo came and told him
As there he stood the stream beholding,
That e'en as Moses made no question,
But to the heavenly voice did listen ;

And when the mandate came, " to sunward,"
Did lead that mighty host straight onward ;
Nor dream'd the sea could stop his going,
With angry waves that host o'erflowing.

So he must leave all earthly finding,
Or ties of home or friend so binding ;
And fearless cross the stream there gliding,
By faith upheld, in God confiding.

So he must join the World's proud striving,
And strike as seen its dark conniving ;
And rend the masks which hide its features
And show how mean are worldly creatures,

And scout its idle pomp and revel,
And soar beyond its wretched level ;
And teach sweet critics, darkly hidden,
To break not silence when unbidden.

To teach them if they've wit or feeling
That which to some needs no revealing ;
They have no right in specious seeming
Their art to ply with malice gleaming ;

They have no right by law that's human
Sly darts to hurl as cankerous foeman ;
All poison'd too from hidden quiver,
And think " call'd out " they'll ne'er be ever ;

They have no right to sit complacent
In scorner's chair, and think it decent ;
No right have they in realm of letters
To sneer at those they know their betters.

To teach them this, and more that's needful,
That echo woke mine ear, all heedful ;
And bade me take the bank uprising,
The stream athwart without surprising.

And to that voice I've since been listening,
And with its tone mine eye is glistening ;
And to the World I've told its warning,
And for the same I've reap'd its scorning ;

And for its witness clear outspoken,
Articulate and full—unbroken ;
And for the olden faith it keepeth,
And that it stayeth not, nor sleepeth ;

And claims to be the Lord's Evangel,
Upholden by his ministering Angel ;
And would not stoop to common level,
Where sense in twilight dim doth revel ;

And hath not pander'd to the notion,
By Science taught, with mad commotion,
That Reason now to age ascended,
The travail of the World hath ended ;

And henceforth is high priest for ever,
Of every lofty gift the giver ;
While Faith is all unfit for sages,
And suits alone the Middle Ages:—

For this, and much of kindred nature,
"The Reader" oped its smoky crater;
And forthwith came the fire outflowing,
And sought to stay mine onward going;

And kindly gave me timely warning,
In the exuberance of its learning,
To keep afar from burning mountains,
Nor e'er approach their fiery fountains;

To keep afar, nor wake its rages,
Concentrated with force of ages;
To keep aloof from such hot crater,
Nor vex so fierce and strong a hater;

To keep aloof, and bore them never
With things beyond their utmost tether;
With words and thoughts of hidden meaning,
Incongruous with their scanty gleaning.

Yet could I hide not my poor offering,
Had sought from mystic gold a covering;
From frankincense and myrrh ascending,
Some sweetness with its substance blending.

Yet was my book, if given boldly,
With loving kindness chargèd wholly ;—
I knew its tone was pure and lofty,
I knew it breathed with music softly.

But fell " The Reader " 'fore my Writing,
And, breathless, 'gan his small indicting;
For that he found a page poetic,
And could not reach its strain pathetic.

O " Reader," thou, the World's great leader,
Thy hand withhold, no more mislead her;
Nor think to stand as interpleader,
When thou hast nought wherewith to feed her.

THE END.

BRADBURY AND EVANS, PRINTERS, WHITEFRIARS.

www.ingramcontent.com/pod-product-compliance
Lightning Source LLC
Chambersburg PA
CBHW020902020726
47497CB00005B/1516